I0594302

HER CONVENIENT
PLAYBOY PRINCE

JAYNE KINGSLEY

BLUEBERRY LANE
PUBLISHING

ALSO BY JAYNE KINGSLEY

ANTHOLOGIES

April Showers: A Seasonal Romance Anthology

Christmas on Hope Street: A Cathedral Springs Christmas
Anthology

STAND ALONE

Loving Lucas

THE STENISH ROYALS

#0.5 Finding a Forever Love (Prequel)

#1 Tailored for Her Prince

#2 A Convenient Playboy Prince

#3 Guarding His Runaway Princess (Coming July 2020)

To my two beautiful daughters.
Also to the corridor outside their room where most of this book
was written whilst waiting for them to go to sleep.

1

"*Y*ou may now kiss the bride."

Lady Sophia smiled as Eva leaned in and kissed her husband, Crown Prince Henrik of Stenaco. The delight on both her friends' faces as they broke apart from the demure kiss was enough to light the whole of the capital—brighter even than Eva's tiara that Henrik had especially commissioned just for today. With an excess of fifty pristine diamonds, that was saying something.

Moisture brewed in Sophia's eyes at the beauty and undeniable true love before her. She blinked away the emotion. Love wouldn't be something she'd choose in her future, she'd seen first-hand how damaging it could be. That said, she was beyond happy that her long-time friend had finally come to his senses and admitted his love for Eva— she was confident *their* love would last a lifetime.

Applause rang out, and Sophia's heart skipped. She plastered a smile onto her face, hiding any of the nerves that threatened to break through. Since this was a nationally televised event, she didn't want to risk the cameras catching her expression being anything but euphoric for her friends.

Particularly since she was originally meant to be the bride in this event—not the maid of honour. A few of the London media outlets still had her cast as the heartbroken ex-girlfriend. How little of the truth they really knew.

The happy couple's marriage did, however, place a slight dent in her requirement to marry. Her stomach churned. That was a problem for another time. Today was about Henrik and Eva, and their wedding that had been a long time coming. Once she heard back from the private investigator about her aunt, she could go back to worrying about her lack of upcoming nuptials and what the devil she'd do about her mother.

Her eyes sought Prince Felix without permission, as they'd done multiple times throughout the ceremony.

Oh.

Slate blue glittered back at her, a smirk hovering around his mouth. He winked at her and Sophia trembled as excitement coursed through her. Felix had always made her shiver —a fact she'd certainly never share with anyone.

For one thing, his list of conquests could stretch across the Pacific Ocean, twice, and she had no time to join that queue. A dalliance of any kind didn't appeal to her right now. What she needed was a husband—preferably one who'd agree to marry her and then leave her the heck alone.

She focused her gaze back towards Eva. The other woman's dress was an art form. Layer after layer of silk glistened with three-dimensional embroidered roses, wisteria, and butterflies. The bodice was fitted, the skirts flaring out in a true ballgown style. Whisper-fine tulle covered her arms, edged with tiny beads. Sophia knew fashion and this was right up there with the haute couture designs she saw each year at the Paris and Milan showings.

Eva turned to accept the cascade of white roses, baby's

breath, and mauve wisteria that Sophia had held for her during the ceremony. The green ivy caught on the silk skirt of her own gown, leaving a miniscule tear in its wake. She doubted if Eva would have noticed if the whole bouquet had fallen to the ground or burst into butterflies. The silly thought turned her smile into a grin.

Sophia followed the newlyweds towards an anteroom where they would sign the marriage certificate and other legal documents. Felix fell into step beside her. He silently held out a handkerchief, his initials embroidered in neat maroon script along one edge.

"Thank you," Sophia murmured, accepting the piece of cloth to dab at her eyes.

"So, do you feel like you've dodged a bullet? You know, since Henrik is desperately in love with someone else." Felix's tone suggested he was aiming for flippant, but he had a funny look on his face. A far cry from his usual assured cockiness.

"I'm not sure if you're trying to be funny or serious, or if you're falling dismally somewhere in between."

"Yeah. Sorry. Weddings make me nervous." He tugged at the high neck of his royal uniform.

"Now *that* I can easily believe." Amusement laced her words and she arched a brow.

"Though for the right woman I'm sure I could change my tune."

"Ha! A likely story, Felix. Given you've sampled most of the eligible women under forty and possibly more besides, I would say you're not about to 'change your tune', as you so thoughtlessly put it." She threw him a sideways smile and was surprised his brows creased slightly.

He caught her eye, the frown smoothing immediately. "What can I say? I like women. And they like me." He stopped walking as they drew alongside the table where Eva sat, taking her turn to sign the marriage certificate.

Now there was the Felix she knew. And the very reason she would never entertain any serious thoughts about him, even if her body begged her to on any occasion that brought them into close proximity. *And other times.*

She shooed the unwelcome thought away. Prince Felix was absolutely the last man she'd consider getting involved with. Not that he'd offered, and nor could she be bothered waiting in line just to fall into his little black book and become another dismissed notch. *No thank you.*

He cleared his throat, the sound warranting a look from Eva who had just finished and came to stand beside them. She gestured that Felix sign next.

"The romance of the wedding getting to you already, hey, brother dearest?" Eva's smile was impish.

Felix sat and scrawled his name on the spot indicated by the priest. "No, no. How could anyone not enjoy an occasion that brings two loved-up souls together. As well as plenty of champagne, good food, music, and gloriously fine women dressed in their best. I look forward to out-dancing you."

It was Sophia's turn to sign the certificate. The others shifted to give her space. She'd felt a little odd that it had been her who'd been asked to take this honour, when Izzie —Henrik and Felix's younger sister—was also part of the wedding party, but Eva had been strangely insistent. Izzie too.

With a flick of her wrist, she signed along the dotted line. She allowed her gaze to wander to Felix's signature. It was flamboyant, yet also elegant—the exact description she'd give the man himself.

She sensed someone move behind her a moment before Felix's head appeared close to her own. His fresh and bold aftershave enveloped her in a way that had her wanting to drag in breaths and hyperventilate. Not a good reaction.

"You know, you're going to have to dance with me too. I promise I've improved since last time. No stepping on your toes. I've had lessons."

Feigning a disinterest she certainly didn't feel, Sophia raised a brow and turned her head slightly. The move brought them even closer. Little puffs of heat spotted her cheek with each breath he took. His eyes held hers, seductive as his focus meandered across her face and slipped to her mouth, almost daring her. To do what? She didn't want to know.

Instead she stood as he also straightened, her heels bringing her into alignment with his eyes which hadn't budged from their assessment of her.

"I wouldn't want to keep you from your adoring fans. Surely there's a young lady out there you haven't taken to bed yet who'll be desperate to dance with you. Far be it from me to stand in the way of that." Her arch tone was a little breathless even to her ears.

She sidestepped around him, curious that his trademark grin didn't quite reach his eyes and he didn't make a return-remark. Sophia moved towards Eva and Henrik, giving them both enthusiastic hugs and congratulating them once more.

The rest of the ceremony—returning to walk down the aisle and standing for countless photographs—was a blur. Her mind had settled back on her own mounting problem. If she didn't marry in the next two weeks, she'd lose a huge inheritance from an aunt she'd never even known about until six months ago.

Just how did Sophia reach the age of thirty and not know her deranged mother had a sister?

Sophia rearranged the skirts of her dress. She was fiddling, something that her mum would be having kittens about if she'd been in attendance. The brief angry text from her was no doubt the reason for her fidgeting. Even absent, her mother ruled her mind. But not for much longer. Now she had a way to escape—had done so for months—that she'd kept under close wraps. But without a miraculous husband it was all going to go up in smoke.

The snarky text from Mummy dearest still shone on her phone screen, almost as if it refused to go away. Guess she was still pissed off that A: Sophia hadn't done as asked and found a way to stop the wedding and turn herself back into the proposed future-princess and B: She hadn't received an invite to the wedding.

Unease burned slightly in her gut that she'd cheated her mother out of attending a royal wedding, but only a smidgen. It was guilt that was born from a lifetime of conditioning. Really she was super thankful to not have her mother here in the flesh. Right now, just seeing that woman made her skin crawl. To think that all these years Lady Cynthia had cosseted the love of such an amazing man—her father—when all that time she'd been cheating on him. How did the woman look at her own reflection without disgust?

Sophia's phone vibrated, the number displayed on the screen knocking the air clear from her chest. She snatched up the phone, sliding a practised thumb across the glossy screen. "Hello?"

"I have news. It appears the last known whereabouts of your aunt can be traced to Ireland."

"Ireland?" Sophia half asked, half repeated. The deep

voice on the other end offered nothing but a grunt. "Where in Ireland?"

"Somewhere up north. I need more funds if you want me to keep looking."

Her heart sank. Why did everything in her life come down to money at the moment? After saying she'd be in touch if she wanted him to proceed further, she rang off.

For all intents and purposes, she was loaded. Except the money wasn't hers. She was nothing but a Barbie doll, being dressed and tossed around by her mother. Cynthia was the one swimming in money, and she made sure Sophia and her father both knew that fact. She also spent stupid amounts of time combing through their accounts and questioning any large withdrawals of cash. Sophia had given up bothering trying to hide where she went and what she spent money on.

But without an actual job, she was stuck. She could ask Henrik for a loan again ... but she was already so indebted to him. The money she'd borrowed to hire this investigator should have given her the answers she required. No way would she waste any more of his money.

She'd just have to find another way.

Sophia had perfected the art of finding another way.

"That's not a happy face. Lucky there aren't photographers—they'd have you drowning your sorrows at your one true love marrying someone else." Eva's eyes twinkled with mischief. She sat at the table with Sophia, her skirts delicately floating out around her.

Sophia brightened at the other woman's presence. "Maybe I should drown my sorrows—you did steal my supposed fiancé. All in the name of true love. I mean, what sort of reason is that anyway?" She winked at her friend. It was her special day and Sophia would not ruin it with her own annoying issues.

Eva performed an over-the-top fake sigh, but her dreamy expression as her gaze found Henrik's from across the room was nothing but one hundred per cent real. Sophia's heart did a little sigh, witnessing such a fleeting moment that held such emotion. How would it feel to have someone in her life who loved her like that? Someone she could share all of her thoughts and worries with, without threat of retribution or scheming?

Of course, that type of love didn't come around every day. It was a one in a million, and Sophia had already met far more than her million—none of them close to *the one*.

"On a slightly more serious note ... I am interested to know why you aren't smiling? We saw you take a phone call ... Was it the investigator? Was he able to find your aunt?"

"Not exactly, no. She's somewhere in Northern Ireland, but that's all he could tell me unless I fronted up more money."

"That's fine. We can arrange another transfer—"

"No. Thank you. But no."

Eva opened her mouth again, but Sophia held up a finger.

"I can't take another loan, and to be honest, I'm becoming frustrated with how long this is taking. I think my best option is to travel to Ireland and look for myself."

"Ireland's not exactly small. Where will you start?"

"Belfast. The investigator said Northern Ireland. I'll call the lawyer and see if he knows anything more. He's based in Coleraine so I could start by asking around there. I'll find something." Sophia glanced around the room at all the elegantly clad couples. The king was dancing with Izzie—which was lovely—though both wore matching strained expressions. It really was for the best that the press had been kept out of the reception. Far too many telling photographs could be taken here. Her eyes zeroed in on Felix who was standing on the other side of the dance floor. His head was bent slightly, his too-long ash-blond hair swept across his forehead. His hands were in his pockets—the whole picture one of elegant sophistication and swagger.

"You two should dance."

Sophia barked out a laugh, swinging back to level her gaze at Eva. "Are you trying to be funny?"

"No. I know you don't think very highly of him, but under that facade lies a truly wonderful soul. I think you two would really hit it off if you let your guard down."

"I think you've had too much champagne and you're seeing everything through rose-coloured glasses. Felix and I are like chalk and cheese."

"Interesting that you knew exactly who I was referring to though." Eva's smile was smug.

Sophia resolutely ignored her friend's last words.

Henrik joined them at the table, pulling a chair over so he could sit beside his wife, his arm cradling her shoulders over the back of the chair. It was such a relaxed picture. Eva had been a fantastic influence on Henrik—previously there was no way that Henrik would have been seen with such informal posture.

"Henrik, we need to send Sophia to Northern Ireland. The investigator has a lead, but she's determined to do the rest by herself."

"Take the plane. When do you want to go?"

"No, Henrik. You have both already helped enough. Thank you, but truly I'll be okay. I'll work out something."

"How?" Henrik's brows raised slightly, but instead of looking condescending he just looked imploring. "You only have two weeks left. Now is not the time to be stubborn. So let me repeat, when do you want to go?"

Sophia swallowed, looking from Henrik's face to Eva's determined expression. He was right, she didn't have time to turn down help so freely offered and without strings attached. They were her friends and just wanted to help. She might want to do this herself, but she also didn't have the luxury of acting without thought. She needed to get to Belfast as soon as she could.

"Now?" She was half-joking, half-serious. Energy coursed through her that would not be set aside; her desire to find her aunt and subsequently a serious chance at her own freedom was enough that it overrode any sensibilities. She was being rude, wanting to leave during her friends' reception, but the idea, now planted, would not let her be.

Henrik glanced at Eva, then back at Sophia. "I shall check it's not required by Father." He stood and walked in the direction of the king. Sophia noted that Izzie was still with her father, though they weren't dancing anymore. They appeared to be having a heated discussion that ended with Izzie shaking her head and storming off and away from the gazebo.

"I'd better go check she's okay," Sophia said, starting to rise.

"No, wait. I'll go after Izzie. Henrik just gave me a nod, which means you need to go pack."

Elation and pure thankfulness filled Sophia. How lucky she was to have friends like these. People who just helped her, and accepted her, without consequence or a third degree—without demanding some form of payment. "Thank you." The words were from the bottom of her heart.

"Good luck. We're only a phone call away if you need help."

Sophia nodded. It was time to find her own destiny.

God, he was pathetic.

Why couldn't he take his eyes off her? What was it about her, specifically, that left him a muddle-mouthed teen whose first crush had smiled at him for the first time? It was lame and he hated himself for not finding the balls to just be honest with her.

But he was playing the long game here.

He shifted his stance. He didn't know why, but Sophia was the one and only woman who had always reached deep inside him and left him wanting to settle down: thoughts that usually brought him out in hives. But he'd dithered, unable to lock himself into any form of decision. That had been until Henrik had told him of his plans to wed Sophia.

Which would have been a huge mistake.

Henrik may not, but Felix remembered a drunken night, just days after their mother's death, when Henrik had opened up about the girl he'd met in Italy. A girl whose name was Eva. He'd professed a love so deep and pure that his words had stuck with Felix. Plus it had been the first time in a while that Felix had felt connected to his brother.

Growing up as the second prince afforded him a lot of leniencies, as well as pitfalls. Henrik would always be the number-one child; their father had been sure that message had been locked in tight. What he hadn't realised was how lonely that would leave him, feeling like there was always this invisible wall between the two brothers.

Felix tried to shake the memories. He'd done the right thing. It might have been an odd way to go about it, but he'd known if he'd just marched up to his brother and told him to marry Eva not Sophia that his brother would never have entertained the idea. Country first; no emotions allowed. No, Felix had made sure Henrik realised his folly for himself, which meant the decision rang true for his proud and straight-laced brother.

Henrik had recaptured his joy and he'd made sure Sophia didn't marry the wrong brother.

Of course, working out how to get her to see he'd be her perfect partner was the ultimate challenge.

For one thing, Felix couldn't even trust his own feelings. He'd always been the fickle prince, the one who'd moved through women and interests like he went through socks. Could he really commit to Sophia and promise never to waiver in that devotion?

His heart had been lost to her for years, but could he truly say that wasn't just because he'd never allowed himself to actually pursue her? Was she just his ultimate quest?

Gah! He was a fool.

She sat there, floating her skirts out about her as she crossed her legs in the other direction. The lilac colour of her dress highlighted her serene beauty to perfection. Her smile tugged at his chest, brightening to a more natural demeanour as Eva sat down beside her. Eva's eyes flicked his way, catching him staring, her brow raised in a knowing fashion. He averted his gaze to the ground.

Yep. Pathetic. And everyone knows of my feelings except Sophia.

"What in the blazes?" He jerked, surprised by the pinch applied to his left buttock.

He cocked a brow at the curvaceous brunette who'd appeared, plush against his side. He'd noticed her watching him during dinner.

"You know that could be construed as harassment in

many countries." He spoke lazily, hiding the annoyance he really felt at being interrupted.

She dipped her head to the side in an artful and most likely practised fashion. Her heavily made-up eyes fluttered at him. "Oops. Maybe you should take me somewhere private so I can apologise."

Once upon a time, he would have fallen for that. But ever since he'd witnessed his brother's fall into the depths of love, he'd found himself left somewhat cold when it came to the opposite sex—Sophia being the only exception to that. This overt invitation left a dusty taste in his mouth. "Perhaps some other time. I'm on duty."

She pouted, not perturbed. "No one will miss us. It's not like you're still required. Lady Perfect appears to be leaving, so you're off the hook."

Her words had Felix spinning, catching a glimpse of Sophia's impeccably coiffed hair and elegant figure moving through the floral arch and out of the reception area. He moved after her, ignoring the indignant shout of his name. He was sure Miss Busy Hands would find some other willing man to entertain her whims. There was only one woman Felix planned to pursue.

Sophia disappeared into the east wing entrance of the castle, leaving Felix with a sense of disappointment. He hadn't even found an opportunity to dance with her.

"For someone who went to the lengths you did, you're certainly keeping your distance."

Felix jolted, taken by surprise again. *Seriously, what is with me tonight?* Normally he was far more on the ball.

Eva and Henrik stood arm in arm—a stance that they seemed to have adopted since becoming engaged. It was almost like they worried if they let go of each other they'd be forever parted again. Felix mentally rolled his eyes at the pathetically sappy thought.

"There's no rush. She's not going anywhere." Felix said.

"Uh ..." Eva glanced to Henrik who nodded slightly "... actually she is. We've loaned her the plane. She needs to go to Ireland."

Shock ricocheted through Felix's chest. "Ireland? What! *Why?*"

Again with the shared, unsure look. What the hell weren't they telling him?

"She didn't explain a lot. But she's looking for someone."

"Well, then, I'm sure she'd like company." Felix jogged off before Eva or Henrik could say anything more.

"Felix!" His brothers voice barked from behind him, but he didn't pause.

There was no way Felix was letting Sophia go off looking for some person without letting her know his true feelings. He'd waited long enough.

2

---

*S*ophia breathed a sigh of relief as she stepped onto the last stair of the private jet. Henrik was an absolute lifesaver for letting her borrow the royal plane. Now she could make this trip without her mother's interference.

Cynthia will be furious when she finds out.

Sophia couldn't find it within herself to mind nor care. Instead, she smiled. It probably wasn't a good thought to have: only daughter taking joy from angering her mother. Except this latest stint had killed any last vestiges of dutiful love Sophia had left.

Cynthia had cheated for the last time. Sophia would make sure of it.

Once she managed to track down her aunt and find out more about this mysterious bequest, she'd be able to afford to tell her father about her mother's cheating ways. She'd be financially free of Cynthia's tight fists. She could continue to run her not-for-profit organisation—Project R—without Cynthia's threats hanging over her head. Her mother ruling her life would be done.

Of course it also meant getting married, but hey. *Don't get ahead of yourself, Sophia*. Hopefully her aunt could be talked around.

The cool air of the plane was a welcome relief from the heat outside. Summer had definitely sprung in Stenaco's capital city, Geravia. She swiped a wrist against her brow, smiling in the knowledge that she would have the freedom on this trip to just sit back and be herself. No expectations to look the part, to be the dutiful lady.

A man cleared his throat, the noise stilling Sophia's heart mid-beat.

"Sophia. So nice of you to join me."

Her head snapped up, straight into the swirling blue gaze of Prince Felix.

"What are you doing here!" Frustration swamped her euphoria, leaving her with the urge to stamp her foot or scream. *Can't I just be left alone to get on with my task?* She did not want to be distracted by the man sitting before her. And he was *all* types of distracting.

Felix stood from his chair, the movement so leisurely and cocky that it just sent her into another spasm of annoyance. Felix could do whatever he wanted, whenever he wanted, and all he chose to do was sleep with women and leave a trail of broken hearts in his wake. So not the person she wanted on this trip with her.

He wasn't her mother; he didn't cheat on someone he'd promised to love and cherish but he was certainly of the same mould.

Or perhaps that was being too harsh.

"I get the sense you're *really* not happy to see me."

It was the grin that brought her undone. One small quirk of his mouth and she couldn't help the answering tilt of her own lips or how her anger just melted to a puddle. Much like her knees were threatening to do.

"Actually no, if you want the truth. Henrik said I could borrow the plane. Apologies. I didn't realise you were going to use it. I'll just ask the pilot to remove my bag—"

"Wait. I heard you were going to Ireland. I have some business there, that's all. I figured there was room enough for us both." His arms spread wide, incorporating the spacious interior that could house at least twenty people.

Of course there was plenty of room for both of them. Yet part of Sophia didn't want to be locked away in the plane with just Felix, for reasons she refused to identify.

But what was her alternative? She couldn't exactly throw him off his own royal plane. She could borrow a car from Henrik and drive to Ireland but it would take days. Days that, right now, she didn't have. Her quest to track down her aunt was timely, with no room for dallying on the way.

"Sophia?"

He'd stood and moved closer whilst she'd been lost in her thoughts, so he was now scant inches from her. Her eyes roved his face, taking in the strong jawline, the dimpled cheeks that had a sparse covering of scruff. For some reason he always looked like the rogue prince he was, did he not shave properly on purpose?

He leaned in close. "See anything you like?" The glint in his eye could power a city for a week.

Sophia huffed. "Really, Felix? Please don't tell me you're drunk."

His only response was to laugh.

Choosing to ignore the waves of heat that were flooding her insides from that one stupid line—of course she didn't see anything she liked—she stepped past him. She'd changed from her bridesmaid dress into something more suitable for travel. The bridesmaid dress was divine, and a part of Sophia had wanted to stay in it forever. The lilac gown was beaded to an inch of its life but felt light as a feather on her body. It had swirled and clung in such a way that Sophia had never felt more beautiful. Eva was beyond talented. But the dress had sparkled far too much, and Sophia had been hoping to avoid any kind of recognition on this trip. Her black tee and jeans were matched back with simple leather brogues. Her snow-white cape coat more for warmth than any sort of fashion statement though the piece still looked stylish. There wasn't an item of clothing allowed in her wardrobe that wasn't the utmost in style.

Thank you, Mother.

At least on that topic they mostly agreed. Sophia did love fashion. But not as much as she loved the legacy she was trying to build and the good she was determined to do for less-fortunate communities.

Sophia flopped into the comfortable leather chair.

"So I'll take that to mean I can give the pilot the green light?"

"Sorry. Yes please, Felix. And sorry for, you know, being ungracious before." She sat up straight in her chair, unable to stop herself, unable to stop the apologies—her manners ingrained into her very skin.

"Ah, there she is. Full Brit back in place. Shame. I was starting to enjoy the slightly less perfect Sophia under that veneer."

Sophia opened her mouth to refute such nonsense but he was already walking to the pilot's door. Besides, it didn't really matter what Felix thought of her. It wasn't like he was ever going to be a likely candidate for marriage. And right now that was all the interest she held for any eligible man.

She took out her phone, planning to catch up on some

social media and any damage control she'd need with her mother. Being in the bad books for not marrying Henrik was still Lady Cynthia Huntington's number-one grudge against her only daughter, but there'd be something else she'd move on to criticising soon. She'd already called Eva talentless which had burned in Sophia's gut. Eva's name was rising within the London fashion circuit and it had nothing to do with the fact she'd just married the crown prince of a beautiful European country.

Scrolling through the messages, one caught her eye. It was from the lawyer who'd initially contacted her months' ago to let her know about the money, requesting an update on her marital status. An update she didn't have. Her eyes scrunched tight against the frustration that flooded her. She wished she had an update, more than anything, but since her agreement with Henrik was thrown to the wayside for true love, as it should have been, she hadn't had time to come up with a plan B.

There was a mere month until she turned thirty-one. The 'time's up' date of her being able to claim this mysterious bequest. Which was why she figured now would be as good a time as any to track down the unknown aunt who'd gifted it to her.

She finished reading the email, knowing she had no answers or proof in response. Her head fell back against the soft leather and she scrunched her eyes tight against the heat and tears that threatened.

Nearly thirty-one-years old, and to the world, she appeared to have the perfect spoiled existence. Her wardrobe was filled with enviable designer gear, her days jam-packed with luncheons and associations with London's elite. Yet what she wanted more than anything was her freedom to just be her. To slip out from her mother's thumb and become her own woman. Surely her aunt would understand her plight? Why else would she have gifted this secret inheritance to Sophia?

Felix paused as he reached the lounge area of the plane. Sophia was seated in her chair, legs elegantly crossed and her face scrunched in pain. His heart clenched at the sight as if locked in a vice. Had he ever seen pain on her face? Or was that defeat? As the thought occurred to him, her eyes flashed open. She stared resolutely at her hands like she was giving herself a stern pep talk. That fire in her eyes was something he'd often woken in the night imagining, but his visions hadn't done her justice. She was a goddess; her ivory skin almost fragile with its pure silky appearance. He ached to reach out and stroke her cheek, her arm. Hell—any part of her.

He cleared his throat, needing to stop the madness of this thoughts. This was not about seducing her with a short-sighted lusty mindset. No. He wanted to delve deeper. He wanted to know why she was the one woman who wouldn't leave his thoughts. He wanted to know if she was the one, the only one, for him. And he would only know that by spending time with her, talking to her. Not just taking her to bed, which was his usual modus operandi.

"Everything okay?" he asked.

Her head popped up from its assessment of her hands, her eyes suspiciously wide like she had been trying not to let tears flow. "Of course. When do we depart?"

"Five minutes. The pilot is just finishing preflight checks. I'll have the attendant bring us some drinks."

"You don't need to wait on me. It's only a short flight and then I'll be out of your hair."

"So quick to dismiss me from your presence, I see. Surely, since we find ourselves alone on the plane together we should use the opportunity—"

Her laughter burst out, interrupting him. "Not going to happen, Felix." Her words mocked him.

No more than I deserve, I suppose.

His reputation preceded him, even if it wasn't quite as bad as the media had portrayed. Still, it hurt that she was so quick to assume that was what he'd been going to suggest. "I was merely going to say we should talk."

"You want to talk?"

"Yes. Why is that so hard to believe?"

Her eyes narrowed in scrutiny, a small frown appearing between those finely arched brows. "Okay. I'll bite. What is it you'd like to talk about?"

"You could tell me why you're hop-footing it to Ireland before the reception has even finished at my brother's wedding. Do you still hold a candle for him?"

"So what if I do? My love life isn't any concern of yours."

"What if I want to make it my concern?"

Again with the laughter. She really knew how to pull his ego down a few notches. Maybe more than a few.

"Don't tell me you've run out of willing women to pursue and you're getting desperate enough to widen your breach to me." She smiled.

Felix had spent enough hours surreptitiously studying Sophia's features to know when she was joking. Her eyes held a delicate twinkle that burst forth. Unfortunately he was rarely on the receiving end of such warm looks.

He swallowed back his desire to just be honest and tell her it wasn't desperation, that he'd admired her for years.

That she featured in his dreams in a way he hoped to make real in the future. But he held back. She'd never believe him.

Instead he leaned in, offering an exaggerated wink. "I'm never desperate. Seriously though. Why Ireland?"

He shoved aside the uneasiness that told him she hadn't outright denied having feelings for his brother. Henrik had sworn that there wasn't anything between them, that they'd never been more than just friends. Their talk of marriage had been a means to an end for both of them, a sensible decision as opposed to any sort of romantic attachment. He trusted his brother had been honest with what he'd told him, but a part of him still pondered Sophia's feelings. She was hiding something—that he knew. Her inexplicable need to get married for one thing. But Henrik and Eva had shared that information with him in confidence, which meant he needed Sophia to want to tell him herself.

The flight attendant chose that moment to arrive with their drinks, informing them they were about to take off. Felix shifted from the seat that faced Sophia's to one that was next to her. The spacious seats weren't exactly close but the proximity had him swamped in a cloud of her perfume. He hadn't a clue what it was called, but it had a delicate floral bouquet that, when mixed with her skin, sang to the blood in his veins. "You'd better buckle in."

"Thanks for the tip. What is that?" She motioned to her glass as she clipped the strap closed across her slim waist.

"It's your drink." Felix took a sip of his own brandy, having developed a taste for it after finding out it was her preferred drink. Silly—yes. He wasn't about to share his reasons for drinking it with her.

"How did you know I drink brandy?"

"I make it my mission to know these things. Now, do I

have to ask a third time? I'm almost starting to feel like you don't want to tell me."

The plane started moving, repositioning towards the runway and then gathering speed.

"I don't want to tell you."

Felix was jarred from his thoughts. "Why not? National secret? Are you really a double-O spy? Gosh, I could totally see that actually. Don't suppose you have a black catsuit in your luggage that you could try on for me?"

She thwacked his arm, then levelled him with a look. "Are you ever serious about anything?"

He grinned, rubbing at the spot. "I'm seriously interested in why you're going to Ireland."

"Okay! You're relentless. How did I never notice that before? I'm going to find my aunt."

His brows shot up. "You have an aunt? Is that on Cynthia or Gregory's side?"

Her lips thinned into a straight line, before she turned to look straight ahead. "My mother's."

Sophia didn't have the best relationship with her mother but like a lot of things, he didn't know the specifics. Her jaw was tense and he itched to reach out and stroke a thumb along her smooth skin, but he didn't think the move would be welcomed right now. She was in turmoil, and clearly finding out about this aunt and going to see her was a part of that. "Is there anything I can do to help?"

Her gaze dropped to her hands which were interlaced, her thumb rubbing an invisible line along her palm. The corner of her mouth lifted slightly as she turned her head to him. "I'm sure you have far more pressing things on your list."

"No. I'm all yours."

Her eyes slid away from his, focusing back on her hands.

"Henrik offered to help too. As did Eva. But I want to do this by myself. It's something I *need* to do myself."

Felix didn't resist the urge to touch her this time. He laid his hand over hers, her movements went still. Her hand beneath his was delicious but he didn't linger, even though he wanted to. He collected his own glass and leaned back in his chair, feigning a nonchalance he didn't feel. Like touching her hadn't just ignited his whole body into flames of want and desire.

He didn't speak. He wasn't able to form coherent words and instead used the icy-cold liquid to bring sensation back to his parched throat. He'd unearthed something about her. It might not have been much, but from her words, this was important to her. And there was no way he was leaving her until she'd met this unknown aunt and all was okay with her.

Besides. His *reason* for needing to go to Ireland was her.

3

─────────

*S*ophia came to with her head cushioned against a warm, strong shoulder, more relaxed than she had been in months. Still fuzzy with sleep, she snuggled in closer to the source of heat. A soft chuckle invaded her brain.

"Morning, sleeping beauty." His voice pushed the last vestiges of slumber from her mind.

She sat bolt upright. She'd fallen asleep. On Felix's shoulder. Bad move. *Bad, bad move.* Now all she could smell was him—an intoxicating mix of masculinity and forbidden desires.

Hadn't she taken great pains to never touch him? To never find herself alone with him? Not because she didn't trust him, but because she didn't trust herself!

She was old enough to acknowledge lust when she experienced it, and her body most definitely lusted after Felix. Which would be suicidal since Felix was a serial dater with a history of discarding women as quickly as he found them. She loved being friends with his family too much to throw that away on one night of pleasure. Even if that one night might just be enough to source her fantasies for the rest of her days.

"Do you know you mumble in your sleep?" he said in a conversational tone.

"I do not! Besides, a true gentleman would never tell a lady such a thing." *Good work, Sophia. Hide behind that stiff Brit persona.*

"Oh, Sophia, we both know I'm no gentleman."

Oh, God. *Down girl.* She needed air—fresh air, and breathing space. To clear her head of the vivid imaginings that were slotted into her retinas. They were *not* appropriate.

Sophia gave herself a mental shake and turned to the window. Outside it was dark but she could make out a tall, glass-fronted building filled with lights. They had arrived. Clearing her throat, she offered Felix a tight smile and then flagged the flight attendant. "We've landed, I presume?"

"Yes, Lady Sophia. We're just waiting on some paper-work to clear and then we'll have you off the plane and on your way as soon as we can."

Sophia murmured a quiet thanks. She hated being called Lady Sophia. Just another thing that her mother could use against her.

"Pole back in place, I see."

"I *beg* your pardon!" Sophia gasped.

Felix's grin widened to the point she wondered if it would split his smug yet stupidly handsome face. "I do not have a pole up my ... my ..."

"Say the word. Live a little."

"Why you—"

His lips pressed into hers, cutting off any further words —cutting off thought. Hell, her brain short-circuited. Prince Felix was kissing her and boy, was she in all sorts of trouble. A kiss this innocent should not feel this good. It should not be sending trembles up her spine and heat straight to her core. His lips pulled back just a fraction, and she shifted forward, following him, needing the connection more than anything. His kiss was like taking a full breath of air after being underwater too long. Her lungs filled with the intoxicating scent that was him. He gently bit her bottom lip, then slid his tongue along the same surface. The move drafted a soft mewl from deep within her. She never wanted this to end. Kissing him was a life-altering experience.

She moaned again. A deeper, heartfelt noise that caught her off-guard.

He broke away, and this time she let him.

"Well, now, that's a turn up." He murmured.

Don't do it. She ignored her better judgement, her eyes flicking to his: slate blue–grey that rivalled the stormiest skies over England. They locked with her own. Her heart skipped. There was not even a skerrick of a mocking glint to be found. She'd been sure he'd kissed her for his own amusement, yet his gaze bored into hers with a seriousness she wasn't sure she'd seen on his face since the day of his mother's funeral.

"No." She said the word without conviction but at least somewhere in the depths of her mind she was still functioning on a human level. The rest of her body was still enjoying lust-stricken shock thanks to Felix's overqualified lip tricks. The man could kiss. And it had only been a nibble.

Imagine if ...

No. No, no, no. She didn't have time to imagine anything. She had a car to collect and an aunt to find, and that was that.

Hooking her Hermes handbag over the crook of her arm, she stood and flattened the front of her skintight jeans

—out of habit more so than need. And, trying to ignore the impulse to go check her appearance—another lifelong habit —she sidestepped past Felix's lazily crossed long legs. Legs he didn't even bother to try and move. She marched down the short, spacious aisle of the plane and offered the flight attendant a polite smile. She'd perfected the art of pretending there was nothing wrong. Years of practise put her in good stead on that front and right now she was thankful. Especially when all of her insides were still going off like firecrackers from that stupid kiss.

They'd landed at Belfast airport and the air held an especially strong fragrance as she jogged down the steps, following the strip lighting. The scent of freedom. Putting the kiss from her mind—easier said than done—she focused on her reason for being in Ireland.

She would find her aunt. Surely she could explain to the woman, who clearly had the good enough sense to keep herself away from Lady Cynthia, that while marriage hadn't quite fallen into her lap as yet, they could come to some other arrangement over the money. It wasn't like she wanted it to squander away on a socialite lifestyle of partying and shopping. She needed that money to buy her independence.

She jumped the last two steps, and looked around, expecting to find her hire car.

Except all that met her in the sparsely lit area was an expanse of empty tarmac. The private plane section of the airport was quite simply bare except for the Stenish royal plane.

She'd been setting aside a few pounds here and there in case a situation like this came up where she needed money that she could use undetected. Her mother never questioned her every-other-day takeaway coffee purchases. The use of the royal plane had been a total saviour, but she'd paid extra to have the car waiting once she hopped off in Belfast.

Flicking her wrist, she noted the time was ten minutes past when her car was meant to be here. It was already nearly eleven. She had hoped to get straight on the road.

"If you're wondering, the car isn't coming." The lazy drawl came from behind her, causing her shoulders to tense.

She spun on her heel, facing the stairs where Felix lolled against the door opening, backlit by the light coming from the plane. He looked like he was starring in a Ralph Lauren campaign—no ... something darker, sexier ... Tom Ford or McQueen. She crossed her arms and cocked a hip, posing with attitude to hide her quaking stomach. What did he mean the car wasn't coming?

Felix pushed away from the frame, leisurely stepping down each stair like he hadn't a care in the world and hadn't just thrown another bombshell into her life. She'd made staying away from Prince Felix of Stenaco a lifelong mission since she'd met him at age sixteen. Even then she'd seen the sparkle in his eye and felt her toes—and other parts of her —curl.

The exact reasons she'd steered clear.

He walked right into her personal space and then had the audacity to lift his lips in his trademark grin. "I cancelled your hire car."

Her eyes snapped shut and she dragged in a deep breath, hoping that maybe her hearing had gone funny. "You cancelled my car?" Her voice was choked, an octave higher than normal.

"Yep."

Hearing not a problem then. She let her head slide back before she opened her eyes, taking in the crystal-clear blue skies. *So much for my run at freedom.* "Why?" Another thought occurred before Felix could respond. "How did you even know I had a car booked?"

Suspicion crept in to replace the quaking. She levelled her glare at Felix and he dodged her gaze. His pulse tick in his throat, and he swallowed. If she didn't know any better, she'd swear Felix was nervous. But that was ludicrous. The man was a lot of things, but he sure as hell was *never* nervous.

"Perhaps I made an error in judgement. Let's go book you another."

Oh, my. He *was* nervous. The question was, why?

"Stop." Her arm shot out, grabbing his forearm which twitched the moment her fingers touched smooth flesh. Her arm tingled. She ached to step in closer and feel more of him. There would be time enough to examine that reaction later—she needed to focus. "What aren't you telling me?"

"Nothing. Let's go. I'll organise you another."

"But how did you even know I had a hire car booked? I only told Henrik and Eva."

She waited whilst his eyes darted over her shoulder and to her forehead, anywhere but directly at her. *What on earth am I missing here?*

"Okay. Truth time. Henrik told me a little about why you're here. Not everything, mind. I was kind of hoping you would maybe fill in the blanks."

Sophia didn't know whether to be angry at Henrik or relieved to have another person on her side. She wasn't certain having Felix in the know was necessarily equivalent to him being on her side though.

His hand grasped hers, the touch weakening her. He'd kissed her. Was this all just some ruse? Was he that bored that he'd decided to set his sights on her?

"I'm not interested in a quick fling, Felix. I'm here to find my aunt because she has gifted me an inheritance but there's a stipulation I can't meet. So I'm hoping to talk her into dropping it."

"I don't believe I was offering a quick fling, but incidentally, why wouldn't you be interested?"

She wrenched her hand away, frustrated that he'd focus on that. Of course he'd focus on that. It was Felix. Bed now, call never.

"Sophia, wait. I'm sorry. You're being serious and I'm having a laugh. What is the stipulation? Maybe I can help you."

"Helping me would start by not having cancelled my hire car! I need that car to go search for my aunt. I plan to start that search in Coleraine, a town that happens to be at least an hour's drive from here."

"You don't know where she lives?"

"Not exactly. Her lawyer was a little light on details."

"Right. Well then, let's go find us a car."

"Us? You are not invited."

"Why not?"

Was he kidding? There were a million reasons why she didn't want him to come along. Number one being the fact he'd kissed her for no reason and hadn't even mentioned it.

"Is this about the kiss?"

She jolted. Had he read her mind? "No."

His right brow quirked, his mouth lifting oh-so-slightly, the whole move filling her with equal parts frustration and lust. Damn him and damn her pheromones!

Felix wanted to press Sophia for details but instead he

waited. Silence would garner some form of response from her. Having cancelled her hire car, he'd counted on her needing his help. Devious? Totally. Required? Absolutely. He wasn't going to be able to win her over if he wasn't in her presence.

Henrik hadn't been keen to divulge too many details via text message about Sophia's trip to Ireland. Or more to the point, Eva hadn't been. He'd been a little surprised that Eva had been the one to tell him he needed to win Sophia's trust and have her open up to him herself. Right now, a few more details would be mighty helpful for his quest.

"Fine. You can come along. Though I don't know why you'd want to?"

"I like your company."

She laughed at him. A great tinkling laugh that had her face sparkling and his guts dropping through the floor. Talk about an ego-crushing.

"Seriously? It's not like we're that close friends—you've never spent more than five minutes hanging out with me alone—only with the rest of the group. What makes you think you'll enjoy this?"

Because I've spent half my life admiring you when you weren't looking. Probably not the best time to own up to that fact though.

"Intuition," he said instead. "Now, let's get moving. Then you can tell me the full story whilst I drive."

She opened her mouth like she was going to argue but then snapped it shut, offering a nonchalant shrug.

He had hoped she'd use his bringing up the kiss to say something about it. Hell, he'd wanted her to acknowledge it had happened, but it seemed she would not. Pity. He might just have to keep doing it until he did get a reaction. He grinned, enjoying that thought far too much.

It didn't take long for Felix to secure them another car. He'd considered requesting the most expensive car they had, preferably something fast and topless, but at the last moment he'd changed his mind. Sophia was here to find her aunt, not to gallivant about the countryside in a fast, showy car. The thoughtful look she'd thrown him after he'd paid for the luxury yet urbane sedan told him she'd been expecting him to go true to form.

Hopefully that had won him some points.

The valet brought their car around and with an ease Felix was accustomed too, they cleared out of the airport. They skirted the city, avoiding traffic and then headed north. The sky was black with night. As the residential lights were swapped out to what he assumed would be green countryside, Sophia relaxed into her seat beside him. Silence had been their travelling companion since leaving the airport and Felix was getting itchy having not spoken in so long. He wasn't used to just sitting quietly.

"Soo ... you said north, but just how far north are we going exactly?"

"Oh, sorry. We're heading to Coleraine."

"Don't suppose you'd be able to pull that up on the GPS? As much as I love driving in the deep of the night with a beautiful woman beside me, my grasp of Irish geography is a little slim."

Sophia fiddled with the car's satnav system, keying in the town name she'd just rattled off to him.

"You know your aunt lives there?"

"No. But that's where the lawyer is based, so I thought I'd ask around in town."

"Couldn't you just ask the lawyer for her address?"

"Also no. She has requested her address be kept private. The lawyer was sketchy on details—he's never even met her.

Apparently it was his father who dealt with my aunt and he's only just taken over the practice. This file popped up on his radar six months' ago when the deadline started approaching and no one had gotten in touch."

"What exactly do you need to find your aunt for?"

Sophia glanced at him, nibbling her bottom lip. He focused his gaze on the road. If he looked at those white teeth delicately folding in those lush pillow lips for any longer, he'd run the car into a ditch.

"You know I run a not-for-profit charity?"

Felix scratched his ear. Not the subject change he was expecting but he was aware of how important the charity was to her, so he was happy to listen. "Yes. Project R. Interesting name by the by."

"The legal name is Project Recycle but a few of my mum's friends would only come on board if the name was hipper. Apparently recycling wasn't a cool enough word."

"Are they your main contributors?"

"Regrettably yes. The clothes they donate auction for huge dollars, which funds my initiative to help children who are forced to work in sweatshop factories and other poor work conditions. We build schools and raise awareness so the community know their rights and aren't taken advantage of. We've looked at branching out into smaller one-on-one funding but it's those big auctions that bring in the cash to keep the charity running. I pretty much do everything. I only have a few other staff members who help out for free. My main help is my friend Rachel who is an accessories buyer in London. It was her intel that sparked the idea and helped us track down the areas that need assistance."

"It's an amazing cause. I'd be happy to discuss with my father how we could be a bigger support? I know Henrik—"

"No. Thank you, but no. I'm not looking for outside

funding. I need a solution to step the business out from my mother's grasp."

"But you just said the business was yours."

"It is. In theory. My mother allowed me to set it up and tolerates my playing with my *little charity* as she calls it, so long as I toe the line and do what she wants. I attend functions she needs me to be at, wear the clothes she wants me to wear, and speak to the right people. In exchange, she ensures my charity doesn't go down the drain. The friends who donate are *her* friends. The people who come along to the auction who have the cash to throw around are from her circle. She wouldn't hesitate to stop the whole thing."

Felix's gut churned, an explosion of red-hot anger threatening to bubble out. "I knew there was a reason I never liked Cynthia." His voice was bitter. How could anyone use their daughter like that?

"You don't like my mother?" Sophia's brows rose, her face a mixture of surprise and delight.

"No." He didn't add that his reasons for not liking Cynthia included her inability to accept Felix wasn't interested in sleeping with her, but he didn't think Sophia needed to hear that. This was just icing on that cake. "I feel like I'm still missing something? If it's just about money, we can make that happen for you. And if you won't take it from us, surely there are others you know who would help too? Can't you change the fundraising strategy?"

"It's not just the money. At least, it's not only that. I need an exit strategy for myself and my father."

Her glance was heavy against the side of his face. Her voice was rife with indecision before it strengthened. She was trusting him. Her demeanour changed and it thrilled him that she was sharing this much with him.

"I caught Cynthia cheating. Again. I'd caught her years

ago, but she'd promised it would never happen again. I was a fool for believing her then but I will be a fool no more. I threatened to tell my dad, and said that we'd leave. She threatened my charity. The money from my aunt equates to eight million pounds. With that kind of money I can walk away. I can house myself and my father. I can set up the charity properly, and spend the time finding new money sources. I can be completely free of her. If she shuts the charity down now, thousands of kids will go without help. I can't let that happen. Whilst I might hate my life, it's a bloody dream compared to what those children experience. I wouldn't be able to live with myself, choosing my happiness over theirs. It's not comparable."

Felix felt humbled. And just a little heartsick. He understood her need to help others—a need he too felt and had never shared with anyone. Only his father knew he travelled to Vietnam twice a year to help with a charity he secretly funded.

For the first time in his life, he could see exactly what it was that drew him to Sophia. She was pure good. She might look like the typical spoilt rich girl, but underneath that she was scrabbling to do everything she could for others less fortunate. She was living a facade, somewhat like he was.

No wonder she laughed at him like he was the royal joker. To the world it appeared he lived a life of squander, riches, and debauchery. He needed to do more. He *would* do more. Starting with ensuring he made Sophia's quest happen. Sophia didn't need to know about the connections he could call on to ensure they found her aunt.

All she needed to know was that he was on her side.

4

*S*ophia's eyes drooped again. They'd been driving for nearly an hour and according to her phone, they should be getting close. Would anything even be open then? "Do you think we should find somewhere to pull in and sleep for the night? It's getting really late. I wasn't expecting you to have to drive the whole way this evening."

"You've read my mind. Though, out of curiosity, what were your plans?"

"I hadn't gotten that far. Probably to just pull over and sleep in the car once I'd exited the outskirts of the city."

"Tsk, tsk. A lady should never sleep in her car."

Sophia aimed a well-placed elbow into his side, with perhaps a little more force than was necessary.

"Umph!"

Sophia allowed a satisfied grin to spread her lips wide. "I hope you're being funny."

"Always."

"I'm pretty sure there was a sign just a little way back that mentioned something about a bed and breakfast?"

"The Irish Clover?"

"Yes. There it is." She pointed her finger. "Pull in here."

Sophia wracked her mind on the state of her personal account. She'd managed to open it without her mother knowing but then she'd used a fair amount of her funds on a little girl and her family who had written to her, and then the car hire ... She hoped there was enough in there to cover her room for tonight. She had multitudes of cards with unlimited spending abilities but under no circumstances did she want Cynthia knowing she'd come to Ireland.

"Do you know you're a little bossy? What if I'd wanted to park elsewhere."

Though she could detect humour in Felix's last words, their meaning shunted away some of her tiredness. "I'm not bossy." Was she?

Felix pulled into the car park where she'd pointed, turning off the engine. "Not always. But you are command-ing. Maybe Henrik's rubbed off on you."

There was an odd note to Felix's tone.

"Why are you and Henrik not close? You used to be ... and I know after your mother died, life changed for you all, but I had hoped you two might have buried the hatchet by now."

"We are close." Felix said quickly, a small frown forming between his brows. He jingled the keys in his hand as he looked at her.

"Then why do you keep getting this odd tone when you mention him, like you're disgruntled with him?" Sophia opened the car door, swivelling both her legs to the side before standing. Just another habit. It wasn't like she was wearing anything that would be revealing. Nor was it likely they'd been followed by photographers. At least she *really* hoped not.

Felix joined her beside the car, two overnight bags in

one hand. He pressed a button on the keys to lock the car before he stepped in her path, blocking her from walking towards the front door. "Not him. Just your feelings towards him."

The words were challenging, his eyes searching hers. She didn't understand?

"I do not have feelings for Henrik. He's my oldest friend. He's the one person I've always been able to be completely honest with, but I swear to you, that is all. There are no unrequited urges and I don't have a secret longing for him. We're just friends."

"But you would have married him."

"I asked him to marry me, yes. I needed a husband. Stenaco wanted their crown prince married. It seemed an easy solution."

"Which I ruined by bringing Eva back. Why do you need a husband?"

Sophia had walked into that one. She sighed, it was time to tell Felix if she was to have any hope of him leaving this subject alone. "It's the stipulation my aunt has placed on the trust money. I need to be married."

"I'll marry you."

Sophia swallowed, the only movement her body was able to compute. Her brain cells dissipated into a wash of emotion, her heart stuttering as a fleeting image of marriage to Felix flashed before her. Three words she'd certainly never thought she'd hear uttered from his mouth, particularly never to be aimed at her.

To hide her initial reaction she pretended to pull on her ear in an exaggerated fashion, hoping to lighten the mood that had settled around them like a thick blanket.

Felix stepped forward, dropping the bags at their feet. He took her hand, pulling it away from her ear, then captured her other hand until they stood, fingers locked together like they were about to raise their arms into a waltz. "Don't play with your ears—your hearing is fine. I said I'll marry you."

Sophia was glad of the contact, sure she would have keeled over otherwise. Shock was infiltrating her body. Inch by inch, it seized her skin. "Why?" Sophia held her breath, waiting for words ... an answer ... Did she really want it?

He had a determined look in his eye but before he spoke, it shifted slightly. "Because you need this. Your charity work, your dedication—it's amazing. And if this is what you need to keep it going, then so be it."

So be it. Funny, but Sophia had really thought Felix had been going to say something else. Something ludicrous. Something that involved feelings and commitment ... which *was* utterly ludicrous. Sophia didn't want love, didn't believe in love. And Prince Felix was certainly the last person in the world who would be able to change her mind on that front.

She stepped away, offering a wan smile that only partially lifted her lips. "Thank you. But no. Let's find my aunt first and hope it doesn't have to come to that."

"But this is an easy solution. We can fly back to Stenaco tonight. I'll arrange the papers tomorrow. We could be married in a matter of days. You could have your money almost instantly. Why are you saying no?"

"I've lived a lifetime in the middle of an unhappy marriage built on lies and deceit. I don't want to put myself into one. Not even for this."

"You were prepared to marry my brother—a marriage that would have been built on a lie."

"No. It would have been two friends who knew being companionable was preferable to love. At least, that's what Henrik thought before Eva came back into his life."

"So you don't think you could find marriage to me companionable?"

"Felix. You're a player. Can you honestly say you'd be content being locked into a convenient marriage with me? I'd be a laughing stock within minutes and you'd resent me. Let's just work on being friends." She smiled, trying to ignore the weird sensation that her words were hurting Felix. Holding back the true reason that she'd never consider marriage to Felix because he was an emotional threat. Putting herself into a loveless marriage with a man like Felix ... she could just imagine that she would end up like her father: a man broken. A man who'd fallen in love with the wrong woman.

There was no way Sophia would be able to resist Felix if they married. And there was no way he'd remain faithful to her. It simply wasn't in his nature.

———

Felix tried not to let the emotional blow show. He was offering her an easy solution and she refused to take it. Because she didn't believe in him. He swallowed back acid. He couldn't blame her. Parental influence could have a huge effect on one's life. His own father had never recovered from the loss of his mother. He was at a distance now that none of them could touch. His mum had been the link that had held them all together. Once she'd gone, having taken her own life, they'd all been thrown into turmoil.

But he'd hoped that this solution could bring Sophia and him together. If they were married, she'd have to spend some time with him. She could learn to see that he was going to change, had already changed. He'd barely been able to look at another woman for months—from the moment he'd heard Sophia and Henrik had planned to announce their engagement. He congratulated himself on his part in averting that mess but it didn't change the fact that if Sophia wouldn't even give him a chance ... he was lost.

"Thank you. For offering." Sophia's words were hesitant. Uneasy silence had opened up after her answer to his refusal. One that Felix had allowed to go on too long.

He winked, putting his grin back into place. He scooped their bags back up and ushered her towards the door, pretending like he hadn't just offered his hand in marriage and been knocked back.

Of course, Sophia didn't know his heart was part of the equation. Probably for the best—he wasn't sure he'd bounce back from that rejection just yet.

The bed and breakfast was a quaint two-storey stone cottage. The foyer was filled with an array of homely furniture, mostly covered in different floral prints. The mismatch was a bit hard on the eyes but the buxom older woman who beamed at them from behind the desk made the rest insignificant.

"Welcome to the Irish Clover. Ye lookin' for a room?"

Her accent was deep, brusque, but also held a sense of warmth that Felix couldn't ignore. "You're a sight for sore eyes. I'm Felix. This is my lovely friend, Sophia. We're after two rooms please."

"Travellin' late for friends." Her eyes did a little sneaky dance between the two of them causing Felix's lips to twitch. "Let me take a look. I only have one room spare. It's a double though, so plenty of space in the bed."

Felix held his facial expression in place but sensed Sophia stiffen beside him. His own stomach dropped. Whilst sharing a room with Sophia was up there on his top ten fantasies list, sharing it when she didn't want to be with him made it pure torture. Still. It was only one night and they had to rest. No way would he allow them to sleep in the hire car.

"Thank you. We'll take it." Sophia made a small noise of protest but he ignored her. She could take the bed. He hoped there'd be a couch or even an armchair that he'd be able to sleep in. He was so exhausted he could probably sleep just fine on the carpet.

He pulled his wallet out, extracting enough pound notes to cover the night and a few extra.

"Room three. Turn left at the top of the stairs."

Thanking the woman with a nod, he took the key and dragged Sophia away towards the staircase.

"I am not sharing a room with you." Sophia's words were clipped.

"You need sleep. I need sleep. What's the big deal?"

Sophia opened her mouth, then snapped it shut. Two pink dots started to form on her cheeks. *Interesting.* Perhaps she wasn't as immune to him as he'd initially thought. Could it be that her issue with this had more to do with her actually being attracted to him?

His mind jumped back to the kiss. She'd moaned, chased his mouth after one small taste.

If he was a lesser man, and just wanted her for one night, he'd use that to his advantage. His body begged him to be a lesser man.

He would not cave.

After walking up the steps, he turned left down the narrow corridor, finding room three. He spun the handle, pushing the door forward whilst he ran his hand along the inside wall, looking for a light switch. Flicking it, the room filled with light. Sophia followed, close at his heels. She breathed a sigh of relief, probably spotting the couch that faced the double bed.

Another sea of floral greeted them, but the couch looked comfortable and that was all that mattered.

"I'll sleep on the couch. You take the bed." Sophia's words were out before he could say anything.

"No. *I'll* sleep on the couch. You take the bed. It's the gentlemanly thing to do."

"Now who's being bossy? Besides, I'm certain you said you were no gentleman on the plane. That's a quick change."

"People can change, Sophia. With the right incentive."

Her eyes went wide; his underlying message had hit its mark. The soft rose of her bottom lip dropped open a little, then she slid it under her teeth.

"Unless you want me to kiss you again, I suggest you stop doing that."

She pulled her teeth away, her mouth drawn into a flat line.

Pity.

Sophia rolled over, struggling to find a comfortable position in the bed. Felix's breathing had evened out ages ago—even on a darn couch he seemed to have no issues going straight to sleep. Whilst she was still in a state of flux. How was that fair?

Ever since he'd made that comment about kissing her, her mind had gone into overdrive. She'd feigned ignorance, accepting the offer of the bed. And after a quick shower and change in the bathroom into summer pyjamas—thankfully she'd packed boring ones that offered nice coverage and a baggy shape—she'd hopped into bed with a quietly murmured goodnight.

Felix had padded about, taking his leisurely time getting ready for bed. He'd stripped to boxer shorts, his bare chest on display as he cleaned his teeth. Sophia had allowed one eye to open, devouring his ripped form, thinking thoughts that one just should not think about a man who was simply cleaning his teeth.

Eventually he'd settled on the couch, a pillow shoved under his head. Sophia had relaxed, her eyes closed, her breathing steady. Except then he'd doused the room into a heavy darkness. Somehow the light had been protective. But with the black night had come hungry thoughts, seductive thoughts. Her mind had played tricks on her, thinking that Felix had stood before walking over to the bed. She imagined him slipping under the covers, removing her silky cotton top one button at a time ...

Him kissing her—every last inch of her coated in his caresses and warm breath.

Stop it!

How easily he'd led her down the garden path. This was why she hadn't wanted to share a room with him. He was far too tempting.

What had he been trying to imply with his comment about people being able to change? She could have sworn he'd meant himself ... but why would he think she'd want him to change?

Why was he helping her ...?

She had totally forgotten about his supposed reason for being in Ireland in the first place.. Unless she was the reason ... but that was ... "Absurd," she whispered the word in the darkness, hoping it would pack an extra punch.

"Absurd is the fact you aren't asleep yet."

Sophia jumped at the husky voice from the darkness. "You were asleep a second ago."

"No, I'm relaxed. There's a difference. It's hard to fall asleep when I can hear your brain going into overdrive from over here."

"My brain is fine."

"I'm a good listener."

"Okay, since you asked, what happened to your task that brought you to Ireland?"

"I'm on it."

"So I was the task?"

"You are the reason I'm here, yes."

"Why?"

"I'd have thought that perfectly obvious."

"Presumably not, since I'm asking."

A rustle sounded before the room was once again lit by the lamp next to the couch. Sophia blinked away at the spots that danced in her eyes. Soft footsteps could be heard, growing louder before the mattress dipped next to her.

Her heart skipped, heat pooling in her core as all her delicious thoughts from before tumbled back into her mind. Was she dreaming? Had Felix read her mind and was playing out her fantasy? The spots cleared from her eyes, landing on Felix who leaned down so he was directly above her. His naked torso was so close that she had to stop the urge to lift up a little and take a taste. His olive-coloured skin beckoned her lips. Heat radiated from him, warming her in ways she could never imagine.

"Sophia?"

She flinched, caught red-handed as she ogled the expanse of skin before her. Her eyes flicked up, only to be captured in pools of lust and desire. She swallowed. "Yes?"

"I'm here because I want to be with you. Now turn off that delicious mind of yours and go to sleep."

Words evaporated. He wanted to be with her? How? As in, just sex? Or more? Did he want a relationship? She tried to push any of the questions through her lips but then she couldn't. Felix's hot mouth took hers in a kiss that went straight from zero to one hundred. She reached for him, her arms locking around his neck. What the hell was she doing?

The kiss rendered her mindless, her body moving without thought. Her fingers clamped onto strong shoulders, massaging the smooth skin, drawing him down until she felt his weight against hers. He fit perfectly. Her leg slid up the coarse hair on his calf, her toes curling in delight as their tongues joined the fray. Had she ever been kissed like this? This was the stuff of fantasy, of losing herself completely in another person. She'd read about feelings and emotions such as these but never had she experienced anything of the sort. Never had she been so completely consumed in a moment. Well, except for the brief kiss on the plane.

His lips broke away. He breathed in deeply. His obvious arousal was stark against her leg.

"We should stop." He voiced the words on a laboured inhalation.

"What if I don't want to?" Had she really just said that? She shifted, pushing her hips up against his length. She ached to feel him, to have him deep within her womanhood.

"Soph ... please." He groaned. "You're going to kill me if you keep doing that." He chuckled, the sound vibrating devilishly down her spine. He raised onto his forearms, almost doing a push-up before he hopped off the bed. His boxers were impressively tented at the front, distracting Sophia completely.

He coughed. "Mind stopping that? You aren't helping a guy out here."

"I can see why you have such a reputation."

Her words were a wet blanket, dousing the mood completely. Felix turned, head bowed and hands slung on his hips.

"Get some sleep," he commanded.

He returned to the couch, plunging the room once more into darkness.

Sophia hated herself. She'd deliberately bated him, then offended him. Why? Because she was scared? Felix seemed ... different. His recent behaviour had certainly been far from what she'd expected, given his reputation.. Just what was the truth?

And what had he meant when he'd said he wanted to be with her?

5

"Yes, thank you, Mother. I am aware of your position."

Felix blinked as the snapped words infiltrated his mind. His muscles protested, as if he'd slept on rock-hard granite, or a pile of sticks. Definitely one stick at least—care of the delectable woman who was tossing biting comments into her phone. He really needed to learn to *not* sleep on his tummy.

How did she manage to look fresh as a daisy? He needed a vat of coffee and a shower. A really, *really* cold shower.

Images of Sophia pulling him into her lush chest assailed him, and his naked torso burned to feel her skin against his. Oh, how he'd love it—her lips moving with his, soft murmurs and moans—his and hers—as he tasted what had always been so far out of his reach.

The look of utter confusion and devastation when he'd called a stop to the proceedings punched him in the gut.

His body may never forgive him for that move.

"*Dammit!*" Sophia huffed, pitching her phone onto the

cushioned doona, closely followed by her own flop onto the bed.

"Rough morning?" Felix croaked. He needed a glass of water. Tossing and turning, and mentally devouring Sophia in his thoughts for endless hours last night, had taken their toll.

"My mother."

"I might need coffee before we continue this conversation."

"There's a pot of tea."

Felix winced. Tea was nice enough, but he needed the stallion's caffeine kick, not the pony version.

Using his right foot, he kicked off the blanket before pulling himself into a seated position. Aware he was still mostly naked and sporting a hefty good morning problem, he stood and strolled over to the pot that Sophia had flicked her hand at. He was satisfied with the audible swallow that came from her direction.

"Could you find some clothes?"

"You weren't complaining last night." He winked, enjoying her discomfort. He wanted to talk about the elephant in the room, not her mother. This seemed as good an opening as any.

"Yes, well. Last night was an apparition. A moment of madness. Which you walked away from, I might add."

Ah. There we go. Was she angry at him? Or sexually frustrated? It was hard to tell. Her face was a demure mask, though her eyes were having trouble staying above his shoulder line. He poured a cup of tea, added a dash of milk, and then took a gulp. The liquid was lukewarm, telling him Sophia had most likely been up for a while.

After placing the cup back on the counter, he arched his

back, stretching out the tight muscles. Now he definitely had her attention.

"I walked away because I didn't want to be hammered with recriminations this morning." He finished the last sips of tepid tea. Crossing back towards where she was reclined on the bed, he leaned in, placing arms either side of her. "When we make love—and have no doubt that we will—It will be because you want it more than anything in the world. No buts. No questions. No thoughts of regret. Only a path forward." He placed a feather-light kiss against the tip of her nose. Her breathing faltered. He pulled away, his grip on his own willpower short. "I'll take a quick shower, then we can find breakfast."

"Wait." She stood, her brows knitted together. Her eyes were a stormy sea of conflicted emotions. "What do you mean by 'only a path forward'?"

"Just what I said yesterday. I'm here for *you*. I'm not interested in a quick bounce around the sheets. I want something more serious. I want you to get to know me. I want to give this"—he flicked his index finger between them—"an actual try." Felix's heart sank a little with each word spoken as Sophia's face slowly fell into a look of bewildered horror.

She shook her head slowly from side to side, like that one movement would be enough to stop him talking. "I don't believe you."

"That's why last night didn't happen. And won't, until you do believe me."

"What if I don't want that?"

His heartbeat skyrocketed. He wanted to glance down to see if the physical evidence of his alarm was on show. He had assumed he'd come up against a bit of a wall. Sophia and he had always sparred and bickered, almost from the get-go. Except that first night they'd met when he'd experienced a mutual attraction that he knew, deep in his gut, was real. An attraction that had scared him, and confused him.

Her apparent choosing of Henrik's friendship and ignorance of himself had led Felix to thrust the feelings into a deep, dark corner of his heart. He'd just fancied her. He had been sixteen—he fancied lots of girls—it shouldn't matter that hers was the name that kept popping into his mind. He'd blocked her from his thoughts, and had taken easier paths. Girls had flocked to him, and he'd done his best to please every last one. But never had any of them touched his heart.

Except her.

If she didn't want him ... well, it wasn't something he was ready to consider just yet.

He grinned, adopting a cocky expression that was only skin-deep. "We'll see about that." He winked, before shutting the bathroom door with a soft click behind him.

Sophia couldn't be sure if she wanted to throw a pillow at Felix or call him back and beg. What the hell was he on about? Where had this sudden about-turn come from? Felix wasn't the type of guy who did long-term relationships, the type to really get to know someone else's every little inner-working. She'd witnessed the revolving door that was his love life and whilst she'd often—okay, more than often—wondered what it would be like to spend the night with him, she'd never seriously contemplated it. Maybe she had last night, but that was an anomaly. That was tiredness and stress. And, well, a body that had melted her brain to a puddle of lust.

He did seem different though. The smug demeanour and assuredness was still there, but underlying all that was a calmer side. She struggled to put her finger on the right word. Determined? No ... decided.

Maybe that was it.

Not that it mattered. He could want the moon for all she could give it to him.

Love was not going to feature in her future. She wanted a husband, but only his name and signature. He could keep the rest. So long as she got her money.

Her phone beeped. She grabbed the offending item, which had only delivered her bad news so far today, and gingerly swiped at the screen. It was a message from Eva, asking how sharing a room with Felix had gone, signed off with a cheeky smiley face.

Heat crept unbidden up her neck.

She started typing in a reply, when she changed her mind, deleting each letter with a tap of her thumb. If Eva knew that Felix was with her, then Felix had told her. And Felix could darn well explain to her why he was talking to Eva about that. Her friend meant well but this whole situation was becoming more complicated by the hour.

There were enough people ruling her life right now. She didn't want to become a pawn in whatever game Felix was playing.

Was Felix playing a game?

She still didn't know what to make of his earlier declaration.

The muffled noise of the shower still hummed through the bathroom door, meaning she had a quick moment to change in peace. She'd had a hurried rinse the night before and didn't think she could trust herself to get naked this close to Felix again. She rifled through her hastily packed bag, pulling out a slinky black maxi dress. Another glance produced a fine striped linen shirt which she threw on over the top of it, tying the tails a few buttons from the base. Slipping her feet into high-heeled sandals, she added a few layered chain necklaces. She looked like she was touring around on vacation. She shoved her hair up into a haphazard bun, leaving a few strands to fall loose at the back.

Her mother had practically shredded her a new one this morning over the phone, demanding answers as to why she hadn't implemented any of her ludicrous suggestions to stop the wedding, picking up from her text-message attack that she'd started the day before. Sophia had deflected with details on what people had worn, trying to remember any titbits of gossip or intrigue that might keep her mother occupied. Status was what her mum cared about. Being at the top. Having her daughter marry the crown prince of Stenaco would have been a real coup. She didn't actually care about Sophia's feelings.

Best not to tell her that she had spent the night sharing a room with the other prince. Nor the fact that that prince had proposed marriage, and implied he wanted something long-term.

Talk about complicated.

The bathroom door swung open, a trail of steam escaping out the top closely followed by a waft of seductive aftershave that left Sophia wanting to fall to her knees and just breathe deeply. "What cologne is that?"

"It's from France. Le Studio Phéromones. Izzie dragged me in there on a trip last year. You can have your own unique *parfum* made."

Hmm. That explained that. Felix personified in a scent. No wonder she wanted to drink it in like air.

Just the pheromones talking. All she had to do was resist and Felix would lose interest. He was a player—he'd show his true colours in the end. No way was he being serious about her.

"What have you told Eva about us?" Her tone was accusing.

Felix raised a brow before slipping a white polo over his head. The move had his stomach muscles clenching, outlining every one of his six-pack abs. Make that eight. She swiped a finger across her lips, checking for drool.

"I told her I was coming to Coleraine with you, to help you locate your aunt."

"Do you and Eva talk often?"

"It's easier to communicate directly through her than Henrik at present. I know they keep each other up-to-date. They are both worried about you, Sophia. As am I. We want to help you. If you're insistent that you'll do this the hard way, then I want to be here. Eva wanted to know how you were faring."

"What do you mean 'the hard way'? Since you seem so all-knowing, what's the easy way?"

"Well, there are two, with differing levels of ease. The slightly harder one would be letting me call my guy to track down an address for your aunt so we don't waste time traipsing the streets looking for her. The easiest path would be letting me cart you off to the local registry and getting hitched."

"You realise for both those options you started with 'letting me'—which isn't allowing *me* to solve my own problem. I turn thirty-one in two weeks. I never solve issues in my personal life. This time, I want to. Is that so hard for you to believe? I'm sick of having other people rule my life!"

He walked towards her before taking her hands. Electric

currents raced from the contact, darting up Sophia's arms straight to her heart. His jaw was almost clean-shaven and she couldn't resist stroking it.

"No. It's not hard to believe. But is it so hard to believe that we only want what is best for you? That *I* want what is best for you? I can see how much you want this. I heard the passion for your work in your voice. I don't want to control you. I just want to help you."

She nodded, not quite trusting *her* voice. For some reason, accepting help from Felix was harder than it was from Eva or Henrik, or even from Izzie.

He'd completely thrown her off balance and she was struggling to find a place to stand where she could find her equilibrium. She ached to accept his help, but something held her back. Rationally speaking, it made perfect sense for her to accept the use of his private investigator. It would narrow her search considerably, but her irrational self wouldn't let her. That part of her held onto the skerrick of hope that she could do something by herself—for herself— just once.

If that made her a fool then so be it. But for once she was taking a stand where she could.

———

Breakfast at the Irish Clover was a full buffet with all the trimmings: eggs, baked beans, sausages, bacon, toast, grilled tomatoes, and fried smashed potatoes. Sophia normally skipped breakfast, just drinking tea until mid-morning when her body seemed to perk up and want food. The spread was enough to turn her stomach a little, but she managed a single piece of buttered toast. Felix piled his plate high like he was suffering from a hangover and this was his only cure.

Unsurprisingly, he finished every morsel.

"I checked with the front desk. We're only about ten minutes out of town. Do you know your aunt's full name? We could ask here if they've heard of her. Innkeepers always seem to be a pool of knowledge."

"Lady Agatha Cromley."

"Are you okay if I enquire?" Felix asked, his voice hesitant.

The corners of Sophia's mouth twitched. He had been listening to her. "Please. I'd appreciate it."

He collected his plate before taking it over to a side counter where other dirty dishes were stacked and walked out of the dining room. He was observant; she'd give him that. The process of clearing up after yourself hadn't gone unnoticed by him and that sort of surprised her. Though it really shouldn't have. Felix might be royalty, but like his siblings, he wasn't ever afraid to do the right and proper thing. Even in this casual, relaxed environment, he fit in.

He cared.

Her musing was interrupted by his return.

He shook his head as their eyes locked. "No luck. Should we go? We'll find the town centre and start there. Coffee shops or the post office."

"You don't think we should go directly to the lawyer's office?" she queried.

"You've already said he wouldn't give you address details. I doubt he'll change his mind just because we're there in person. People at cafes love to chat. Plus, I need coffee."

Sophia shrugged. She was a tea drinker through and through, but the penchant for coffee ran strong in all three royal siblings. There'd been coffee at the breakfast buffet, but clearly it hadn't met Felix's exacting standards.

"Let's go," she said, draining the last of her tea.

Sophia was almost sad to see the back of the little bed and breakfast. The owners were delightful and whilst she wouldn't call the night relaxing, she had slept surprisingly well considering the bombshell that Felix had dropped in her lap.

"If we follow this road, it turns into the main part of town. Did you want me to drive?"

Felix glanced at her. "I'm fine to drive. Maybe you can tell me more about your charity. I wasn't aware that it was something you wholly ran and funded. For some reason, I assumed you'd have a team helping you and investors."

"Let me guess: you had me more as the girl who did lunch, shopped and made occasional important phone calls?" She battled to keep the bitter edge from her voice.

He threw her a suspicious glance. "No. I know you don't just lunch and shop. You forget, Sophia, that I know *you* better than you think. I do actually pay attention."

She felt suitably chastised. Edginess from her mother's conversation still hung over her head and she was taking it out on an unfair source. Or was it that she wanted to push him until this new Felix cracked and reverted to the old Felix? The one who had always twirled his grin about but had never paid her any real attention. The one who wasn't a threat to her carefully protected heart.

"The charity came about because I couldn't stomach the abuse and waste that was going on in the world of fashion. Don't get me wrong—I'm a big believer in the arts and supporting growing talent, but once I started on the fashion council board it became clear that not all businesses were being run ethically. I couldn't sit by and watch people being abused and underpaid for the hard work they were doing. I started to get to know a lot of people in the industry and they talk. Some of the stories were just unbelievable. Eventually I managed to take a trip to some of the countries in question, on the pretence to my mother that I was accompanying my friend Rachel, who buys accessories for a chain store in London. What I saw ... it was heartbreaking. There were kids as young as seven, part of a family team, sitting in a windowless room gluing beads into earrings. No ventilation. I could barely breathe from the fumes. The wages were a pittance. Not livable standards by any First World country's means. I just couldn't not do something."

"That's admirable."

"No. It's human. I have spent my life feeling like a puppet on a set of strings. I was sick of not contributing. I fought my mother about studying, going out, and getting a real job but she wouldn't hear of it. Oh, I could study, but work was for lesser people. My only role was to be her Barbie. Set to marry the richest and most influential Ken. By the time I realised that was her end goal, well ... it was too late." *I had become a coward by then.* She opened her mouth to voice that thought out loud but stopped herself. Was she ready to share to that level? Share how stupid and pathetic she felt that she'd allowed herself to become this ... tool?

Felix flicked her a quick glance. She wasn't ready but that one look helped, an unspoken offer of support.

Sophia dragged in air. "This was something I could do. I came up with the idea, using my mother's friends to start a twice-yearly auction, selling off their outcast fashions to raise money. I managed to make it seem like my mother had concocted the idea and all of a sudden money and support flooded in, with a click of her fingers. It's been far more successful than I'd imagined."

"If your mother is so dysfunctional and controlling, why hasn't your father stepped in? Can't he help you? Set you up so you're independent?"

Sophia snorted. It wasn't ladylike but who the heck cared. "The money is my mother's. *All* of it. She runs it like Fort Knox. She's a money-hungry, scheming, bitch. And she's got my father wrapped around her little finger." She could almost taste the fury in her voice.

It drove her mad how much her father put up with.

"That's quite the character assessment. Though it doesn't surprise me." Felix cleared his throat, his fingers tapping the steering wheel.

"You not liking my mother wins you big brownie points. Everyone else seems taken in by her—why aren't you?"

He sucked in a deep breath, before letting it whoosh out. "I need to tell you something that I'm not sure you'll like."

"If it's to do with my mother, I assure you, nothing can shock me."

His eyes were unreadable as they skimmed her face before they returned to the road ahead. "Your mother has propositioned me. For sex. Twice."

She'd been watching his face, his Adam's apple bobbed, and she almost wanted to laugh. "You mean you haven't slept with her?"

He threw her a frown.

"Sorry. That was uncalled for. I appreciate you telling me. But to be honest, I'm not surprised. It's come to my attention recently that she's bedded half of the eligible men in London. You're certainly her type."

Sophia's eyes drifted out the window, taking in the view. Lush green grass whizzed by on either side, dotted with the occasional house. Felix's admission didn't shock her, but it niggled more than it should that her mother had propositioned *him*. Like it was a more personal attack than any of the others. She was inordinately pleased to hear he'd turned her down. Why was that?

Because I want to sleep with Felix.

There—she'd admitted the truth—if only to herself. Heat coiled through her chest and slithered downwards. Her body twitched as Felix shifted in his seat.

"I'm sorry about your mother. The way she's treating you …"

She turned to him, waiting for him to continue, focusing on his words and blocking out her unwanted thoughts.

His mouth tightened. "I wasn't aware that she was practically blackmailing you into submission. I couldn't begin to imagine how that must feel."

His words sent a shiver of warmth down her arms, like a gentle caress. She had someone else on her side. Only very few people knew the true extent of the emotional turmoil that her mother had caused. Having Felix aware of it broke one of the small barriers she'd placed between them.

"Thank you. I trust you won't share the information around. She's threatened to cut me off more times than I can think, which doesn't bother me, but the idea of her shutting down the charity stays my course. I can't walk away when she has the power to do such damage. It sucks, but it also seems very 'First World problems' compared to what others are dealing with."

"Did you actually just say 'it sucks'? Who are you and what have you done with the utterly proper Lady Sophia?"

"If you weren't driving, I'd smack your arm right now."

"Didn't stop you yesterday. Besides, you can take retribution later. I really hate it when you kiss me—that would be a terrible punishment."

The glint in his eye was obscene. As was the thrill that accompanied his words.

"Truth. Why me?" She wanted answers before she gave in to the strong desire to do just as he'd requested.

She focused on his profile, on the strong cheekbones and slightly scruffy jawline. How had that returned already? She wanted to reach out and stroke her fingers across the tiny pins of hair, just as she'd wanted to touch the same spot when it had been clear earlier.

He didn't reply. Would he ever? His fingers clenched and unclenched around the steering wheel.

"Do you remember the first night we met?"

Sophia's brows knit in confusion. "I was at the palace for your sister's birthday afternoon tea. It was her fourteenth birthday, I believe. Why?"

"That's not when we first met."

She wracked her brains. She was sure that had been the first time she'd met Prince Felix.

"The night before, you were at a party. I found you outside. You were hideously drunk, unable to stand, and nearly puked on my shoes. You were wearing a pale pink beaded dress. Sort of vintage-like, very fitted and short. You hated it but said your mother had made you wear it. She made you go to the party, where you didn't know anyone, so you could meet the 'right' sort of people."

Recognition dawned, hazy snippets of that night coming back to her. "That was you?"

"Yes."

"I don't remember a lot. I do remember waking the next day in my hotel room with a horrid hangover and no recollection of how I'd made it back. My shoes were neatly placed at the end of the bed. That was you?" Her throat was tight, her words a little strangled.

"Yes and no. I paid security and housekeeping to make sure you were delivered to your room, sight unseen, and put to bed comfortably."

"You were sixteen. And you thought to do all that? For someone you'd only just met?"

"You left a mark. Even then."

His actions floored her. "Why didn't you say anything the next day?"

"Because that night, you said your mum had sent you to the party to meet a prince. The next day, you and Henrik were glued to each other's sides. You didn't so much as smile at me. So I figured you'd made your choice."

"And now?"

"Now it's time for you to make the right choice. I was the first prince you met, after all." He threw her a wink, but she could sense there was something missing from his face. His fingers were still fidgeting against the steering wheel.

"You know Henrik and I have only ever been friends. Nothing more."

"I do know that."

"Why did you pretend to date Eva?"

Felix flicked the indicator on, the rhythmic ticking quite loud in the charged silence of the car. He pulled off to the side, gliding the car to a slow stop. He shifted to face her, giving her his full attention. His eyes searched hers, deep and with a magnetic pull she couldn't ignore. "I needed to bring Eva back into Henrik's life. I couldn't let him announce his engagement to you. I couldn't stand by and watch you marry someone else."

His words reverberated around in her head, bouncing like a pinball machine. Lights were scattering everywhere in her mind but she was struggling to hold on to any. His dating Eva had been about her? Henrik had told her that

Eva and Felix had only been pretending but he'd never said why. And she hadn't asked.

"This is a lot for me to take in, Felix. You must understand why I'm completely thrown by your words. You're literally referred to as the 'Playboy Prince' in the media. Yet here you are, sitting before me, telling me you've held a candle for me all these years and want this to become something real? I just don't think I can believe you."

"I know." He nodded. His voice was solemn. "It will take time. But that's why I'm here. I have all the time in the world to prove to you I'm serious."

"What changed though? Why now?"

Had she ever craved a concrete answer so much in her life? This didn't fit in the little square box labelled *Felix* that lived in her mind. Time ticked past, the clock flicking over digit by digit.

Is he ever going to answer me?

6

Felix didn't exactly know how to explain his change to Sophia. It had been gradual: witnessing his family start to crack into pieces after their mother's death; watching Henrik become an untouchable force, almost devoid of life; observing Izzie perform outrageous activities, date completely unsuitable men, all to get their father to acknowledge she still existed. His own behaviour ... he'd buried his grief in alcohol and a whirlwind of affairs, discarding each as quickly as the next arrived. He'd travelled the world—New York, Paris, Vegas, Sydney—on a drunken mission to forget his grief. Yet the moment he'd witnessed Henrik's change in demeanour, seeing the weight lift from his brother's shoulders, something inside him had also clicked. He was tired of living his current lifestyle. He wanted to fill the hole that had appeared in his heart. And something told him that Sophia could be the person to do that.

He didn't want to be the predictable larrikin of the family. The playboy prince who no one took seriously. It was time he stopped looking, hiding from real truths. It was time he grew up.

But how to tell Sophia that without her thinking this was just another phase? His whole life he'd struggled to make people see him as anything other than the back-up prince. The second son. The guy who made you laugh, but not the one you really listened to. And he'd been okay with that. In fact, he'd played to his strengths. It suited him to hide behind that smokescreen persona. But was that really who he was? Deep down?

"Are you ever planning to answer me?" Her voice held a slight edge, like she was trying to remain patient but was finding it hard.

"Yes. But it's not like I had a near-death experience and made a sudden decision. This has been a gradual change. I haven't been with anyone in months. From the moment that Henrik told me you two planned to announce your engagement, there hasn't been anyone. That news, it shocked me. I'd never believed the rumours that you were an item. I looked for Eva. I contrived to bring her to Stenaco—to get her back into Henrik's life. I won't apologise for that, though I know it has caused problems for you."

"Is that what you being here is really about? Penance?"

"No! I'm here because I want to spend time with you. I've already told you I'll marry you. I can solve your problem with a single phone call."

Sophia muttered something that sounded decidedly like 'don't want your bloody help' but Felix chose not to ask her to repeat it. She was folded up in her chair, her shoulders hunched inwards, her arms and legs crossed. Her whole persona spoke volumes. Until he could convince her he needed to just back off. Except he didn't really have a concrete answer. But he did have time. And he would help

66

her see through his actions that he was here for the long haul. He was serious about turning this into something.

He slotted the car back into gear, pulling out onto the road. They drove in silence. Houses and buildings gradually swapped out the countryside. Felix looked about as they drove down the main street. Just how long would it take for them to find any sort of detail about one Lady Agatha Cromley. It wasn't exactly a tiny village.

He parked close to the town hall, and switched off the ignition. "Are you angry at me?"

Sophia let out a small sigh. "No. Of course not. I'm just confused. And I'll admit, I'm a little stressed." Her eyes flicked to his. "I might have been a little hasty in taking this trip, being so sure I could just waltz into Ireland and find my aunt."

"Needle in a haystack, perhaps?"

"Maybe a pencil."

"Say the word and I'll make a call."

"Any particular word?" She offered a smile, and at least this one appeared a little more normal—less forced that those of this morning.

"I've always loved the word *kiss me*."

She levelled him with a look. "That's two words. Let's go. My aunt won't find herself."

They walked down the cobbled road in the direction of the town hall. Felix hooked a finger against Sophia's hand, drawing it into his own. Warmth spread up his arm from the contact. Had he ever just enjoyed holding another woman's hand before? It almost seemed pathetic how much joy this one manoeuvre gave him.

An elderly man walked past and Sophia stopped him with a smile. "Excuse me, can you please point us in the direction of a good coffee shop?"

"Aye, luv. There's one down this street and to your right. But I'd recommend continuing two more blocks and then turning towards the river. There's a place close to there called A Baan Tale—best coffee in town."

"Thank you, so much."

"No, thank you. Your smile is going to delight my mind all day long."

A noticeable rosy tinge appeared in Sophia's cheeks. If the man wasn't close to double his age, Felix would have stepped in and marked his territory. As it was, he was enjoying Sophia's reaction to the compliment too much.

They continued walking, her gaze fixated on the ground before them.

"I don't think I've ever seen you blush."

"I don't. Normally."

"The delights of Ireland getting to you?"

"It does feel different here, somehow."

"Probably the company."

Her cheeks had returned to their normal colour, as evidenced by the droll look she threw him. "How do you maintain that level of confidence? Surely it's exhausting."

"Same as how you maintain your façade, I imagine. Years of practise."

Her brows quirked, the little confusion lines appearing between her brows. "I don't have a façade."

"You do. But it's fading since we've been here. You're normally more ... prickly. And very formal."

"You're normally not so deep. At least not with me. Is this how you romance other women?" Her voice was light, teasing.

His jaw tightened. He tried to accept her words as they were clearly intended, but it hurt that she thought this was still part of his 'routine'. "No."

She squeezed his hand. "I've offended you."

They rounded a corner, the path mainly filled with other couples casually strolling towards the river. He spotted the coffee shop the other man had spoken of. It had a few tables out the front and a deep green awning. The rows of two-storey town house buildings that surrounded it looked old but somehow inviting.

The shop only had a few spare tables, giving Felix a visual confirmation that they did a decent trade.

"I'm not offended. I just have a way to go with you. But I'll get there." He winked, his equilibrium balancing out. He was never one to allow himself to stay down for long.

They entered the building, Sophia grabbing the open table in the window whilst he placed an order for an espresso and English breakfast tea. He tried not to wince at the amused smirk of the shop assistant.

"I'll bring them out."

"Thank you. Don't suppose you've heard of a woman called Agatha Cromley? She'd be in her mid-sixties?"

The woman pursed her lips and for a moment heat sprung in Felix's chest. Had they got lucky?

"Nah, sorry, love. Not heard that name in these parts and I've been here long enough. Has she lived here a while?"

"I'm afraid I don't know. I've never met her. That's her niece by the window. We were told she might live here. Thanks anyway."

Felix sat across from Sophia. "No luck."

Sophia slouched in her chair.

"Don't give up. We can go for a wander around. Maybe once you've been walking for a time in those heels, you'll come to your senses and marry me."

"Ha! Just the walk I think."

"Can't blame a guy for trying."

The coffee was lifesaving for his taste buds and his brain synapses. Being around Sophia, he needed all the help he could get. Unlike with other women, where he didn't care two hoots what he said, with her he was on guard, always searching for the right thing to say—searching for the right way to convince her to give him a chance. It was ... eye-opening.

If their trip around Ireland continued for much longer than today, Felix would have to call in favours with Izzie. The nine missed calls from his assistant this morning told him that he was in the bad books and missing events he probably should have considered for longer than a microsecond.

"Aren't you going to be missed today? I'm pretty sure Eva said the post wedding brunch would be followed by official family photos."

"Do you read minds as well as enslave hearts?"

"Whatever that means. I'm serious. You have duties back home you shouldn't be shirking this way."

"They can Photoshop me in."

"You aren't taking this seriously."

He captured her hand in his, holding on tight when she went to pull away. "I am taking this seriously. Right now, I'm exactly where I need to be. Henrik and Eva know and understand."

"And your father?"

"He'll forgive me. He's used to my gallivanting off."

She seemed to ponder his words for a moment. He figured she'd pull her hand away. Instead, she shifted it slightly to return the hold, her thumb resting over his. Something inside him twisted—a feeling that he'd never experienced before, a wholeness that had been missing.

"Tell me something about Prince Felix that no one else knows."

"Okay. I hate olives."

"That's ridiculous. Not good enough. I want something serious."

He went silent for a moment then answered in a carefully neutral voice. "I miss my mum. I worry that losing her has broken something in the family that can't be repaired. Especially in Izzie."

"Izzie? I know she was devastated at the time but she seems okay now. A little wild perhaps. But nothing unusual for a princess with the world at her disposal."

"It's more than that. She's ... become unreachable sometimes."

"Are you worried she's like your mum?"

"No. But I worry she thinks she is."

"Have you asked her?"

Felix let out a scoff. "Izzie takes the cake when it comes to being stubborn and not listening. Pushing her to talk when she doesn't want to will only send her further off the edge."

"So what do you plan to do?"

"For now? Nothing. I'm keeping tabs on her. There isn't much else I *can* do until she chooses to open up."

Felix waited for Sophia to finish her last sips of tea. They'd fallen into a companionable silence. It gave Felix hope that she still hadn't pulled her hand away.

"Should we go for a walk? I wouldn't mind heading towards the bridge and seeing a little of town. The River Baan is meant to be quite pretty."

"Sure. You're the boss."

They strolled out of the cafe and turned left towards the

river. A light breeze in the air ruffled the fringe across his forehead. Sophia tilted her head back a little, as if she was soaking in the sunshine and fresh air. Strands of her hair had escaped the messy up-do she had going on. He had a strange urge to tug on her hair-band and let the rest of her hair hang loose. This slightly more relaxed version of Sophia suited her.

Being here with him suited her.

At least, he thought it did.

They meandered along, occasionally stopping people and asking if anyone had heard the name Agatha Cromley. They walked the bridge path, pausing at the halfway mark to take in the view that spread out before them. Water flowed underneath the bridge, the distance making every-thing below look miniscule. By silent agreement they leaned against the stone railing and just watched the water flow past.

Felix itched to speed up this search by getting in touch with his private investigator. She wanted to do this herself, he understood that and she'd explained her reasons but he still ached to just step in and help—safeguard her from whatever would happen if they didn't track down her aunt.

"What's plan B?" Felix asked.

"I don't have one. Yet." She laid her crossed arms on the railing, resting her head to the side on top. Her eyes fluttered shut for a moment, her lips parted in a soft smile.

He mentally captured the image. It would never leave his mind from this point forward. "You are truly beautiful."

Her eyes stayed closed, but her brows quirked in a way that told him she didn't believe him. She straightened, her eyes flicking open again. "What do you think we should do next?"

"I think you should let me help you."

"I've already said marriage is off the table for now, Felix.

I'm so close to finding my aunt. I can feel it in my bones. We just have to keep looking." Her voice held a hint of desperation.

Her tone ate at his resolve. She wanted to do this her way but what would it hurt if he set his investigator onto the hunt as well? He surreptitiously pulled his phone half out of his pocket and quickly tapped out a message before hitting send.

"I didn't mean marriage. I understand your thoughts on that. C'mon. Let's head back into town. We could go check out the church and town hall. Perhaps some of the staff who work at those locations may be able to help us. We haven't tried the post office yet either."

His phone vibrated indicating an incoming text. His man would be on the job. Unease at his taking this step was fleeting; Sophia needed answers. He'd help her do this her way, but if they didn't find what they needed, then his backup plan would.

Sophia slumped down into car. It was late afternoon, and Sophia's feet were starting to ache after having walked around in heels for most of the day. "We're not getting anywhere, are we?"

Her question was rhetorical and she was glad that Felix didn't comment. Her hope from earlier had all but dissipated. Her idea to traipse around town asking if anyone knew an Agatha Cromley now seemed silly and foolish. The town's population exceeded twenty-five thousand. Had she really thought this would work?

But what were her options now?

Marry Felix? It wasn't that the idea was unappealing. It

was that she was scared. Scared she'd commit herself to him, and that he might want her now but what of next month? Next year? She hadn't told him everything. The marriage had to be validated for five years. Would he really be able to commit for that long?

Did she trust him? Did she trust she wouldn't lose her heart to a man unable to commit?

She'd never wanted to marry—her parents' example had only left her with a bad taste in her mouth. But what was more important? Her freedom? Her happiness? Or her heart?

"Should I find us somewhere to stay tonight?" Felix was watching her, an odd expression on his face.

"You think I'm being crazy, don't you?"

"Is that a trick question? It feels like a trick question." He grinned.

"No. I'm serious. If you were me, what would you do?"

"I'd lean over and kiss me. Because, how could you not want this." He flicked his finger indicating his torso and then circled his face.

"Serious doesn't feature in your vocabulary does it?"

"Seriously? No. But I think you need to do whatever feels right. Do you want to give up looking?"

No. She really didn't want to give up. For once, she wasn't going to just give in and go along with her mother. She wanted to fight for this.

She shook her head. "Let's go find some food. Afternoon tea always helps."

An incoming call sounded throughout the car. Felix pulled his phone out of his pocket. He glanced at the screen, and the corner of his mouth tightened. He hit the red decline button.

"Who was it?"

He dropped the phone into the centre console and shrugged. "No one."

Sophia didn't buy his response for one moment. She picked up his phone, swiping up to see who had rung. There were various missed call notifications but one name stood out.

"You have a lot of missed calls from ... Gollum? Who is Gollum?"

He cleared his throat, his eyes zeroing in on his phone in her hand. "Uh, I really meant to change that." He winced, collecting the phone.

"So?"

"It's George."

"Why have you got your assistant's number under Gollum in your phone? That's kind of ... cruel." She frowned. George did have a strange resemblance to the creature from *The Lord of the Rings*.

"But true. I can see you making the connection."

"No way. I'm not admitting to that."

"You should see his gleeful expression when he's around my father's crown."

"I feel like you're trying to distract me now."

He sighed. "Okay, you're right. I was only kidding. I'll change it later."

"That wasn't who called just now though. Who was it?"

He looked at her, his eyes roaming her face like he was weighing his options before replying. His pulse throbbed in his neck. He was hiding something from her.

"Felix?"

He shook his head. Was he frustrated with himself? Or her?

"It was a private investigator."

Oh. "You've hired one." Her voice was flat.

"Yes."

As much as she didn't want to ask, she had to admit that her current plan held exactly zero chance of success. "What has he found?"

"I'm not sure. You can listen if you like? It's your choice, Sophia. I know you wanted to do this your way. I promise I'm only trying to help. I'm not trying to take control." His voice was strained.

Her anger retracted at his words. He was giving her the option. How often did that happen?

"Yes, please."

He tapped a few buttons, his message bank connecting. A man's deep voice filled the car. "Prince Felix. I have the address you requested." The voice rattled off a street name and number. The town name was not one Sophia had heard of and definitely was not where they were currently looking.

Felix ended the call, rubbing his finger across the screen in a circular motion.

"My aunt's address."

"Yes."

"Not in Coleraine."

"It would appear not."

Charged silence took over the car. Felix swallowed, opening his mouth to speak and then shut it. He tossed the phone back into the console.

"Okay." She nodded. At herself as much as at him. "Can we go now, then?"

"To Donegal?"

"You said you were here to help me find my aunt. It appears that's where we're going to find her."

He pulled his seat belt into place, waiting for her to do the same, and then indicated to pull out onto the road. She wasn't sure, but her reaction seemed to surprise him. Did he think she'd get mad at him? Part of her was still ticked off at his taking action without consulting her, but bottom line: she didn't have the time to argue over how they found her aunt. So long as they found her.

That was all that mattered right now.

7

"It's a two-hour drive to Donegal from Coleraine. We might have to put off visiting your aunt until tomorrow unless you want to turn up in the evening," Felix said.

"I don't think I can sleep tonight now that we know exactly where she is." Sophia glanced at the car clock. It was just after half past three. "It will only be around five-thirty when we get there. That's not too inconvenient a time usually, is it?"

"I'm not sure I'm the best person to ask. I don't exactly answer our front doorbell."

Sophia bit her lip, for some reason finding the image of Felix answering the front door of the Stenish royal castle highly amusing. "Do you have a front doorbell?"

Felix shrugged; the move was casual but there was a ghost of a smile at his lips. "I actually have no idea."

"Why don't you have bodyguards like Henrik?"

"I used to, when I was younger. But I kept leaving them stranded in foreign countries or ditching them to go to places I wasn't meant to. My father would lecture me. I would ignore it. Eventually, he saw my point. I wasn't the crown prince; I didn't need nor like being watched like that. I think he eventually realised that I wasn't worth the protection."

"Is that really how you see yourself? Not worth protecting? You're still a royal prince."

"I might be born royal, but I don't think anyone will ever see me as a royal prince who could rule a country. It's not where my strengths lie."

"I think you're selling yourself short."

"No. I know I'll never rule. And nor do I want to."

"So what do you want to do? Where are your strengths?"

"Government relations. I'm good with people. I like travelling." He glanced at her, a small frown between his brows. "I actually fund a charity as well. I've never told anyone else this—the only other person who knows is my father. I support an orphanage in Vietnam. I go visit twice a year. The kids don't know I'm from a royal family, or that it's my money that keeps the place going. I just get to hang out and be an everyday person."

"How can that possibly not be public knowledge?"

"I have photographs from other trips doctored, dates changed etc. It all gets sent to the media."

"There really is a lot about you I've never known."

Felix had a depth she'd never known about, but he'd also never denied his penchant for women. Not once in his track record had he stuck with one. What the heck was so special about her? *Nothing.* Her mother's spiteful voice sounded in her mind, causing Sophia to shiver. She blanked the memory.

As the car ate up the kms towards Donegal, Sophia's edginess rose. With each bend they rounded, she was one step closer to her goal. Would her aunt like her? Would she help her?

The house at the address was a cute, two-storey stone building with a sloping roof and high windows that sported pot plants on the sill. She swallowed, her mouth dry, her gut churning. Taking a deep breath, she gave herself a mental talking to. *You* can *do this.*

"Would you like me to come?" Felix asked.

Sophia pursed her lips, considering. On the one hand, she had no idea what to expect, and turning up with someone else might go against her. After all, her aunt obviously valued her privacy. On the other hand, the idea of having Felix's physical support by her side was like a warm comforting hug. One she couldn't turn down. Not today.

Offering a small nod, she pushed open her door and stood on the path that led to the house. The garden was full of blooming geraniums, dahlias, and asters. It was a picture of health and clearly well kept. A car was parked alongside the house in what appeared to be a side lane. Hope leapt into Sophia's heart that someone was home. Surely that was her aunt's car.

Felix's matched her stride as she marched up to the door and rapped her fist against the wooden surface with more force that she'd originally planned. The noise echoed a little before Sophia registered movement on the other side of the door. It swung open to reveal a woman, she guessed a few years younger than herself. Confusion had her mind fumbling for words. "Hi, I'm sorry to bother you. I'm looking for Agatha Cromley. I was informed she lived at this address."

The woman frowned. "Oh dear. Are you friends of hers?" Her eyes travelled to Felix and widened a little before they returned to Sophia.

"I'm family. Her niece."

"Oh!" Shock spread across the other woman's face before it was replaced by a sort of sadness and strain that left Sophia's heart sinking to the ground.

A little girl appeared behind the woman's skirts, an impish grin lighting her face.

"I'm so sorry. She said she didn't have any family. Would you like to come inside?" The other woman opened the door wider but Sophia didn't move, her legs seemingly melded to the spot. Something about the tone and her expression told Sophia she wasn't going to like anything else this woman said.

"No. Thank you. Has my aunt moved?" she asked, clinging to a final shred of hope.

"Gosh, this is a bit awkward. I'm so sorry, but Agatha passed away. A week ago. She sold us this house just before it happened. I asked to keep in touch with her. She seemed so nice but sort of sad. When she said she had no family, I felt compelled to check in on her. Her death came as a shock."

"What happened?" Felix asked.

Sophia was glad he'd asked. Her brain had stopped computing. She swayed. Felix's arm came around her waist, pulling her against his side. His thumb stroked her hip, the only thing she seemed to be able to focus on. Her eyes drifted from the woman and child before her, concentrating on the cement steps beneath her.

Words came as if from underwater. Her aunt was dead. Cancer had taken her quickly.

Was she okay?

Was that question for me?

Sophia looked up. Two sets of eyes stared at her. One questioning, one concerned.

"I'm sorry," she whispered, shaking her head, before turning and walking back to the car. She hopped in, staring resolutely ahead. Just what the hell did she do now?

She tried to focus on her initial problem, blocking out the fact that a woman she'd never even known, but had been closely related to, had died. How was that fair?

No, stop thinking about that. One problem at a time. If she had no way of asking her aunt to change the stipulation—and since she wasn't into seances, that option was now definitely out—her path swung straight back to marriage.

Felix will marry you.

She shooed the thought away.

Maybe she could pay someone to marry her?

Except she didn't know or trust anyone enough to go that route. What if it was reported as a fake marriage? What if someone then tried to take the money away from her? The lawyer had said if the money remained unclaimed it would go to the state. If the marriage didn't check out for five years after the marriage date, the money would have to be returned. Eight million pounds was a tidy sum. The stipulation would be followed up on.

Was it wrong to pay a stranger to marry her to claim money from someone she'd never even met? And never would? Except she'd have to pay them handsomely ... five years was a long time.

Felix.

As if thinking his name conjured him, the driver's-side door opened and he slid into the leather seat beside hers. "Are you okay?"

She wished people would stop asking her that. No, she wasn't bloody okay. But she couldn't afford to break down now. "I never knew her." Her voice was stilted.

"I don't think that matters. She was still family. It's all right to be upset by this news."

"It doesn't seem ... real."

Felix didn't answer. Instead, he turned on the car, waited for her to do up her seat belt, and then drove off. To where, Sophia had no idea. Mindless driving appealed to her, lost as she was in her own head.

She leaned against the window, the glass cool against her cheek. Houses slid past her view too quickly for her to take in details. Felix appeared to be driving aimlessly along street after street, until they started to all merge into one. Sophia scrunched her eyes tight, ignoring the lone tear that slid down her face.

The car slowed, driving over speed bumps before it stopped. Sophia's eyes flicked open. They were in a car park. A white wooden railing blocked the car from going farther up the incline of a grassy hill that was covered in headstones.

"Is my aunt buried here? Or do you just have an urge to visit a cemetery?"

"Your aunt is here. I thought it might help."

Sophia turned to Felix, her brows knitted in question. How would coming here help?

He switched off the ignition. He reached over and collected her limp hand from her lap, lacing their fingers together. "When my mum took her life, it didn't seem real. I was told what had happened. I was told what the official royal statement would be. But it was like I was standing next to my body, like I was in a dream, watching the situation unfold for someone else. It wasn't until the funeral, seeing her name on the gravestone as her casket was lowered into the ground, that it sunk in. A wave of emotion crashed down on me. I have never known such sadness, as if I'd put on a thick wool coat that was sodden with water. My body has never felt so heavy. I struggled to move my limbs. I can still hear my sister's broken cries. I can still feel that burden."

Sophia was rooted to the spot, Felix's words reaching her in a way she didn't know how to deal with. She'd been at the funeral, but she'd stood beside Henrik. She'd been wracked with sadness. The queen had been beautiful inside and out. For her to take her own life had been a terrible tragedy, and one she'd deeply worried about in regards to how it would affect both Henrik and Izzie. She'd seen Felix, his face a little pale, his eyes flat. But he had shed no tears. He had seemed to be coping.

Even then she'd avoided seeing the real him.

"Sorry. I didn't mean to burden you with that or go into such detail ... I just thought that maybe seeing the grave would help you in some way. Maybe it was a stupid idea. We can go."

He went to shift his hand away but she gripped his fingers tight, refusing to let go. "Thank you. For sharing that. And for bringing me here." She eyed his profile, keeping her gaze on him, willing him to turn her way.

Turbulent blue eyes swung towards her. He was always so good at hiding behind that fun and flirty persona that she hadn't realised what was hidden beneath: a man who cared. A man who felt life just like everyone else. A man who wanted a chance with her, if she was brave enough to risk it.

Snippets of that first night from years ago floated back, of him holding her hand, stroking her forehead. She'd been struggling to understand this new Felix, yet now she knew he was that same boy from her memories it made more sense. They had been total strangers yet she could remember feeling safe with him. Not once had he tried to take advantage. He'd been a true gentleman.

But it was more than that. He was a good man, and Sophia was starting to realise just how far he would go to help those he cared for. Did she want to take that risk? Did she want to see what this burning attraction could lead to?

She dropped her gaze to his lips.

"You've had a shock. Do you want to go?" His voice was a little strained.

It took Sophia a moment to answer. "No. I'd like to see it."

They walked around, heading towards the newer area. It didn't take them long to locate the headstone with Agatha Cromley written across the top. It was simple, nothing to indicate she came from serious money. Looking at her aunt's name, at the birth and death dates, all she could think was that she'd never get answers.

"The lady back at the house told me Agatha was a lovely woman. She'd wondered at her not having any family, since she'd seemed a bit skittish when she'd asked. I'm so sorry, Sophia. I know this wasn't the ending to your trip that you hoped for."

A lovely woman. One who Sophia ached to have known. Of course, people referred to her mother as being a lovely woman too. And she was far from that.

Had it all been a smokescreen on her aunt's side as well? It was possible Agatha had been just like Cynthia—obsessed with money and desperate to keep it to herself. Sophia couldn't justify the thought. If Agatha had been like Cynthia, no way would she have created the trust.

Whatever her intentions, Sophia would never know.

Felix watched Sophia. Her normally milky-coloured skin

was ashen, her posture slumped. She looked ... beaten. The grave before them was proof that she couldn't change Lady Agatha's mind on the trust stipulations. Would Sophia take him up on the offer of marriage now that she had no other options?

He hated himself that that thought brought him even an ounce of joy, that she'd have to turn to him.

He could understand her reservations. His track record didn't speak highly about his motivations or his long-term probabilities. He also knew now wouldn't be a good time to repeat his offer.

"There was a cosy-looking pub just back up the road. Can we please go there?" Sophia asked.

He didn't let the surprise at her words show. "Pubs have alcohol. I shall never say no to that."

Her eye-roll told him he'd hit his mark. When in doubt, he fell back to his flippant ways. He'd shared a part of his soul in the car and had been left reeling ever since, trying to find a patch of steady ground to stand on. She'd looked at him ... differently. Like she'd started to see him, the real him, for the first time. And it scared him as much as it excited him.

If he wanted to prove he was serious, there was no way he could let the scared part show. That was a sure-fire way to send her running in the opposite direction.

Sophia started back towards the car. Felix went to fall into step beside her but paused, spying a little patch of tiny blue flowers growing a few metres past the grave. He jogged over, plucking a few before he returned to lay them in a little pile on the grave. It was a pathetic offering, but it somehow helped to know he wasn't walking away leaving the grave empty.

Sophia had stopped walking, her face unreadable as he

rejoined her. She took his hand, the move easing the unfamiliar ache in his chest.

The pub was small and smelled of dark ale and overused deep-frying oil. Felix breathed deeply, drinking in the familiar air. Sophia didn't look as impressed, and stood out like a sore thumb. In what he assumed was her idea of casual, she looked like a bloody princess. It was the blonde hair, blue-eyed perfection she exuded. Even with her sparkle dimmed, she still lit up every room she walked into.

God, I'm corny.

"Why did you do that?"

"Bring you to a pub that you requested to be brought to? Gee, not sure." Felix played dumb. He knew Sophia was referring to the flowers but for some reason he didn't want to focus on that right now. Seeing the grave had brought to mind memories he'd much prefer stay buried in the depths of his heart.

"All right. My first shout. What do you want?"

He stilled her hand. "Let me get the drinks. You choose somewhere to sit. Brandy?"

"Yes." She hesitated before a small sigh escaped her mouth. "Thank you."

He placed their orders and waited as the bartender poured a small glass of brandy and another double shot of whiskey over ice for him. He would limit himself to just the one drink, but he needed it to hit him where it hurt. The strength of the Irish whiskey would surely do that.

Sophia had chosen a cosy booth against the stone wall. The fabric covering the seats had a small tear and a handful of unidentifiable stains that Felix mentally shrugged at. Her back was ramrod straight, her mouth grim.

"Thank you," she murmured as he pushed her glass into

her hand. "I seem to be saying that to you a lot at the moment."

"I'm not complaining."

"You seem amused though. Why's that?"

"You look uncomfortable."

"Seeing me uncomfortable amuses you? That seems ... mean."

"I meant you having to say thank you to me—a lot—was making you look uncomfortable. Why is that, I wonder?"

"I don't like being indebted to people. You more so than others."

"Why me more so?"

"Because I feel like you'll call in any debts accrued."

He leaned closer, waggling his brows a little. "Can the debts be collected as kisses? If so, pay up, my dear."

She scrunched her nose before throwing the contents of her glass back in one gulp. "I'm going to get another."

Felix started to object but she was up out of her chair and heading towards the bar, her hips swaying in a way that had the words drifting off. He wasn't the only one noticing either. The bar didn't have a lot of patrons but those there were mainly men. And all were focused on Sophia.

Perfect.

He hoped she didn't plan to drink too much. A repeat performance of when they'd first met wasn't really what he had in mind for tonight.

8

_____

*S*ophia's head was beginning to spin a little. Was this her fourth glass? Or maybe her fifth? She should have kept better count. The bar was starting to fill, table space becoming thin on the ground. They should really think about finding somewhere to sleep tonight.

Her mind had registered that Felix hadn't ordered another alcoholic drink after the first round. He'd switched to soda water. He hadn't said a word about her apparent mission to dull her pain with brandy, for which she was eternally grateful. Her phone vibrated in her pocket, as it had been doing on and off for the past hour. It would be her mother.

It was an instinctive knowledge. Even countries apart, Sophia felt trapped by that woman.

Feeling decidedly brave—though it was probably a false bravado—she pulled the phone out, swiping the screen.

Bingo. Three missed calls, two voice messages, and five text messages.

The last message indicated the height her mother's

anger had reached. Taking a deep breath, she clicked on the first message.

'Sophia why isn't your picture in the papers from the post-wedding brunch?'

Oh no.

A hand plucked the phone from her fingers. "Not sure reading messages from your mother right now is such a good idea."

"How did you know it was from my mother?"

"You get certain crease lines in your forehead when it's her."

"Really? No, never mind that. She's questioning why I missed Henrik and Eva's post-wedding brunch."

"Ignore her. They knew we wouldn't be there."

"Yes—but … we were part of the wedding party. It's going to look highly suspicious that neither of us were there! My mum is asking why there weren't photos of me. How long do you think it will take for the press to put two and two together and come up with twenty-seven? They'll say we've run off together."

"We have run off together."

"Not like that we haven't!"

"We could though. The offer of marriage is still there. It would solve a lot of problems."

Sophia's thoughts scattered. He was serious. Spending every moment in Felix's company these past two days had given her an insight into him that she hadn't before taken notice of. His varied facial expressions were at the top of that list. He mainly held a lazy smile, perfectly at ease, his nonchalance clear in every line of his face. But he also had a serious face. One he adopted when it was time to get something done. One that was clear on his face right now.

"It would solve problems for me, yes. But how would

marrying me help you? Be serious, Felix. There's a large jump between you deciding you want to dabble in dating and committing yourself to marriage."

"It's only a piece of paper. If things don't work out, we walk away."

Her cheeks heated and she scrunched her fingers into tight fists, her nails bitting into her smooth flesh. How could he be so careless? Marriage wasn't just a piece of paper. It was a commitment to another person. A promise to be faithful. That was why the agreement with Henrik had been easy. There were no feelings there. There had been no chance that she'd fall in love with Henrik.

"No. Just no."

A group of giggling, loud women burst through the doors of the pub, resplendent in vibrant pink, sporting tiaras and feather boas. Felix turned in his seat, taking in the commotion like most other patrons. Sophia took the opportunity to escape to the bathroom. She needed a time out to get her thoughts back together.

Her balance was a little off, but she did manage to walk/stumble into the loos. Leaning against the sink area, she took stock of her appearance: not a hair out of place, make-up still pristine. Considering her emotional-self was in tatters, she'd expected to find some evidence on her outer-self. That just seemed ... odd.

She pushed back from the counter, regained her balance, and then tugged at the neat twirled bun. Bobby pins flung to the floor in her haste but she didn't bother to collect them. *Plenty more were they came from.* Her hair tumbled in a mass of blonde waves and random curled sections about her face. She shook her head, finger-combing out sections. The result was immediate and far less formal. With the slight glassy sheen to her eyes, she looked kind of ... sexy. *Even if I do say so myself.* She giggled.

Time to be serious though, Sophia. What the hell do you plan to do now?

She'd considered multiple situations for this trip. What she'd say to convince her aunt to help, ways she could talk her around. She'd had a whole spiel about her charity, how she planned to use the money, guarantees that it wouldn't be frittered away. Not once had she considered not finding her aunt alive.

How awful that must have been ... dying so suddenly. It didn't sound like she'd had anyone with her in the end, but Sophia hoped that she hadn't been alone.

Blue eyes skipped into her mind, alongside a cheeky grin and salacious wink.

The answer to her problem.

Her eyes closed, heat burning behind her lids as tears threatened. Whatever option she chose, there were pitfalls. If she didn't find a way to secure the money, she'd be stuck with her mother—stuck in this endless loop of doing her bidding. Unless she found herself a husband who would possibly break the chain, but as yet, no one had made her heart beat faster or sent shivers down her spine. Well ... no one except Felix who did all those things and more.

But wouldn't marrying the one man who did pose a threat to her heart put her in a situation that was far scarier? What if she fell for him, and he walked away?

Her eyes flung open.

She'd just have to make sure she didn't fall for him.

Sophia nodded at her reflection. Now seemed as good as any a time to discuss Felix's offer. And not just refute it outright without seeing what he thought of the information she *hadn't* shared with him. Like the fact it couldn't just be a quickie marriage and divorce once the funds were in her bank.

Five years was a long time to consider monogamy.

———

Felix drummed his fingers against the wooden tabletop. Sophia had been in the bathroom a long time. He rubbed at his chest, trying to ease the tightness there. Was she okay? Today hadn't gone to plan. Sophia was reeling, and had mainlined brandy in a way that would be concerning for a seasoned drinker, never mind a featherlight slim woman who'd already experienced a wave of shocks. She hadn't eaten a whole lot today either. Neither of them had.

The waitress pushed a bowl of chips soaked in gravy onto the table.

The heavenly smell assaulted his senses and grumbling stomach but he would wait for Sophia to reappear. Fingers crossed, his casual reminder of his offer of marriage hadn't sent her hightailing it out the bathroom window.

Five minutes more. If she hadn't reappeared by then, he'd go find her. It wasn't like it would be the first time he'd detoured into a women's bathroom.

Fingers tiptoed across his shoulders. *Odd.* Normally he'd have felt her presence. He started to turn just as a buxom woman fell onto his lap.

"Helloooo, handsome. Has anyone told you that you have a remarkable resemblance to Prince Felix of Stena ... um, Sten-something. I can't think of the country name now." Her giggle was high-pitched and grated a little on his eardrums.

Oh, man. He did not have time for this.

"Prince who?" he answered, with a grin. A half-hearted one to be sure, but it seemed to do the trick.

The woman let out another peel of laughter. "I have a problem. Can ye help?"

Her finger started exploring again, this time tracing the buttons of his shirt. His smile dipped with every inch. This was getting bloody uncomfortable. He caught a whiff of strong alcohol—rum, if he wasn't mistaken. He'd bet his entire royal fortune that this woman was drunker than a sailor on payday.

"Maybe we could take this conversation outside. I think you need air."

He stood, holding her side so she didn't topple over. He hadn't bargained on her flinging her arms around his neck and practically climbing him.

"Kiss me," she slurred.

He dodged the puckered red lips, which caught the side of his cheek and ear. A fact she hadn't seemed to realise.

"What the hell, Felix?"

Spinning towards the voice, his heart sank. Sophia stood before him, her hair in glorious waves. She looked like a warrior princess with a determined expression in her eyes that was fast sliding into dissolution. This looked bad. Really bad.

"You say you'll marry me—that you want to help me out? Yet here you are having found a willing woman in three seconds flat." She flung an arm out, circling Felix and the woman who had slid back to the ground but was still clinging to his side. "I can't trust you. You can take your offer of help and shove it where the sun doesn't shine."

"Wait!" He stepped forward but was hindered by the dead weight clinging to him. Darting through the crowd with ease, Sophia stormed her way out of the bar.

"Was that your girlfriend?" Drunk woman had found her voice again.

Felix used his shoulder to wipe away the sticky residue at his cheek. His shirt came away with red smudges. "Not exactly. Chances are certainly a lot slimmer now." He helped the women to sit in the spot he'd just vacated.

"I'm really sorry. I'm at my friend's hens party. This was a dare. I've ruined something for you, haven't I?" The drunk woman's eyes stared blearily back at him.

How little she knew. She sounded genuinely contrite though, and Felix couldn't bring himself to blame her. This task was never going to be easy, and nor should it be. Nothing in life worth fighting for ever was. "Can I get you a glass of water? Or walk you back to your friends?" He held in a sigh. He needed to go after Sophia but this woman could barely stand. He couldn't just leave her, as much as his body was itching to run.

"Can you find me a clone of you? I just ruined your date and you're being so nice to me."

He focused on the woman before him. She was pretty, with a cute smile. A year ago he'd have jumped at this chance. But now? It just felt wrong ... she wasn't Sophia. If that wasn't proof he was ready to commit himself wholly to one woman then what was?

She was still looking at him, waiting for an answer.

He winked. "I'm one of a kind. C'mon, I'll take you to your friends." He slung her arm over his shoulder and lifted her in his arms, spotting the group of women in pink who were all wearing various expressions of shock, amusement, and delight. There were a few catcalls and whistles as he carried her over to her friends. Depositing her back with her party, he declined an enthusiastic invitation to stay.

"I have someone I have to find."

"Is that the blonde who ran out of here?"

"Yes. She's the woman I'm going to marry. Wish me luck, ladies!" With a cheeky grin and bravado that was only skin-deep—it did nothing to blot out the utter dread that had struck his heart—he jogged out of the pub with whoops of encouragement following from behind.

The air was cool outside, the sun having disappeared hours ago. He flicked a glance at his watch. It was nearing nine. *Where could she have gone?*

He checked the car but it was locked, the keys still safely in his pocket. Wherever she'd disappeared to, he hoped she'd gone on foot. He'd have a better chance of finding her if that was the case.

The path to the left led back towards the cemetery and something told him she wouldn't have chosen that way. He took off to the right, jogging along the path past closed shops for half a block, then across a road until the buildings became residential.

The town was fairly small, the streets mainly straight. Reaching another intersection, he spun on the spot. He could still see the pub in the distance, and nothing but dark road in the other distraction. Which meant if Sophia had come this way she must have gone down a cross street, or been running full pelt. He squinted, spotting what looked like a children's play park about halfway down the street to his left. He started walking, feeling more confident with each step that the park was where Sophia would have gone. As he moved closer, he heard a creaking noise, like that of a swing.

He ran, pausing only when he reached the gated entrance to the park. There she was, gently swaying to and fro on the swing. She was leaning back, her gaze toward the night sky. She didn't appear to have heard him. The only noise was the squeak of the swing each time it swung backwards.

"Sophia?"

She jerked up, stopping the momentum of the swing with her feet. "Go away, please."

Her voice was tiny, and he struggled to hear it. Ignoring her request, he unlatched the gate and walked over to sit on the swing next to hers. "No. I won't go away until you hear me out. What you saw back there—it wasn't me."

"I might be a little tipsy, but my eyesight is just fine."

"Okay. It was me, but I didn't instigate it. I didn't encourage her. She's on a friend's hen's night. It was a dare. I swear to you, Sophia, I am *not* lying. I haven't thought of another women other than you in months. You are the reason I am here. I meant it when I said I'd marry you."

"And stay married to me?" She paused, then looked up into his eyes.

She'd been crying. The sight broke something inside him. He ached to take her in his arms but he sensed moving any closer would only scare her away. He'd lost a lot of ground after what happened in the pub. She was like a scared animal, ready to flee.

"I wasn't entirely honest about the stipulations. That's why I haven't just paid any old person to marry me. I need someone to stay married to me for at least five years. Otherwise I risk the trust being closed and having to return the money. The law firm has been instructed to do checks. You're a high-profile person, constantly in the spotlight. We can't just marry to get a piece of paper and then you have your fling of commitment only to get bored and return to your old ways."

"You don't believe I can do it? That I can stay committed to you?"

"I believe that I need to be totally sure nothing would harm this deal. What if I get the money, free myself from my mother's grip financially, and you screw up? What if the money is taken away? I'd be left with no way to support the charity."

"I would never leave you high and dry like that. I've already told you, I could invest my money. You could walk away from your mother tomorrow if that is your deepest wish?"

He sensed his words weren't taken well. Her shoulders slumped, her eyes closed but not quickly enough that he missed the pain etched in those blue waters.

Why was she so against accepting his help? What would it take?

"I want to be able to do this by myself."

Her voice was so quiet he had to lean in to catch her words. Almost like she'd said them to herself, not to him.

"Taking money from an aunt you've never met isn't exactly doing it yourself." He hated himself the moment the words left his mouth.

"No. I guess you're right."

The night air offered no comfort for his stupidity. He needed to show her he could do this. Giving up now would only prove her point. "Funny that you came here. It's like we've circled back to the night we first met."

She cocked her head to the side. "I guess so. I do feel a little tipsy still. Though I promise not to vomit on your shoes."

"It's okay. You missed my shoes last time. Though I can't say the same for the owner's gardenias. Whose party was that anyway?"

"I don't remember."

Laying his hands on his knees, he pushed to a standing

position. Taking the few steps to close the gap between them, he then knelt in the bark chips in front of her. "I'm sorry. Sorry for your loss today, sorry for the words I said just now. Sorry for so much that I can't even put it into words. But at some stage, if you want to break free of your mother, you're going to have to accept help from someone. I am kneeling here, promising to help you. I will marry you. I will stay by your side until you order me to go. You just need to take that step, to trust me."

9

*S*ophia's heart stumbled, threatening to stop. Her breathing facilities certainly had.

How could she say no to that? Felix made it sound so simple, so easy ... to just trust him. A cool breeze ruffled the hair at his forehead. Unable to stop herself, she flicked it off his brow using an index finger.

"I want this to work for us," he whispered.

Sophia teetered on a ledge, his words the last push she needed to fall.

Laying her palm against his cheek, she leaned down and kissed him.

Sensible options be damned—she wanted to feel those lips against hers. She wanted to tremble in his arms and leave all her worries behind. Kissing him would do that.

He groaned—a guttural noise that dragged her from lazily wanting to full-on desperation in moments. Her fingers dove into his hair, drawing him closer. The silky texture was divine under her hands, and she massaged his scalp, wanting to feel every inch of him.

He tilted his head back farther, changing the angle of the kiss with expertise.

Marrying Felix would be no hardship. Even trusting him seemed plausible at this moment. What worried her more was giving her heart to a man who could shatter it into a million pieces.

He pulled a hair's breadth away. "Marry me."

His lips hovered just out of reach. She leaned in to close the gap but he shifted, dodging her.

"What is this? Pleasuring me into capitulation?" She murmured.

"Is it working?"

"You might need to try harder."

Her lips parted in greeting as he closed the gap once more, her words proving to be highly incentivising. After dragging her to a standing position, he wrapped her arms about his neck before hitching her into his arms. She clung to him, bringing them into such close contact as to leave no question of his desire for her.

Sophia wished they were in a room, somewhere private. She wanted Felix. She needed to feel him everywhere and have him block out every decision she had to make. For once, she wanted to just experience being with him—to think of him and only him.

This time, when he pulled away they were both left gasping for air.

"We need to find somewhere to stay." He lowered her gently to the ground and Sophia was left a little dizzy.

"I just need a minute."

"I'm potent. I know."

His grin sent her heart into further flutters. This so wasn't fair. No wonder women fell at his feet all the time— that grin should come with a health warning. Not that she'd be admitting that to him. "Not as potent as my heels combined with brandy."

He glanced at her shoes, as if noticing the heels for the first time. "Why do you always wear heels?"

"Too much time out of them means it's hell to pay when I next have to wear them for hours on end."

"I'm sure there's logic in there somewhere that makes sense. Hop on. I'll carry you back to the car." He spun, presenting his back to her.

"You're going to piggyback me?"

"Yes."

"That's ... crazy, yet oddly sweet."

"You can repay the favour by rubbing my back later."

"Always a catch with you, isn't there?"

"You'd be bored if there wasn't. C'mon. Jump."

For some reason she did, without hesitation, the move bringing her mind back to his offer. "Okay. Let's get married."

He stumbled a little, nearly dropping Sophia to the ground. "If I'd known offering to piggyback you was all it'd take, I'd have done so earlier."

"It wasn't that. You're right. I need help. You're offering to help. It should be easy." Her words were light, and his back stiffened beneath her. Had he been hoping she'd declare she was desperate to marry him? That she trusted him whole-heartedly? These feelings and changes in Felix still felt out of the blue ... She was desperate for more time to explore them, to spend time with him without this hanging over her head, but that wasn't a luxury she could afford. There were less than two weeks until her birthday. She needed to be married before then.

She wanted to be married before her mother could throw some stupid birthday party and parade her around.

By the time she was thirty-one, she wanted to be long gone from her mother's presence, hopefully with her father in tow.

"I'll call my lawyer tomorrow and have him organise the paperwork."

"Okay."

"Any preferences for a big splashy wedding?"

She laughed. "You're joking, right?"

"Guess so, given your reaction. We'll cross that off the list."

"I figured we'd just get a special licence and go to town hall or a registry office?"

He didn't comment.

Shifting to pull herself a little higher on his back, she peered around at his face. His mouth was tight, his brows drawn down. Was he unhappy that she'd turned down the idea of a big wedding? "Was, uh, the big wedding something you wanted?"

"Nope."

So that's a yes then. Confusion taunted her. Why would he want a big splashy wedding? Was he trying to prove something? Surely it made more sense for them to just get married on the quiet and let the news filter out slowly. She wasn't daft—they wouldn't be able to keep the information from spreading like wildfire eventually but she figured they didn't need to make it a huge shebang.

Stenaco had just held a royal wedding, one for the ages. It had been the most beautiful wedding she'd ever attended and perfect for her friends. But not what she'd choose for her own, should she ever have her dream wedding. Which she wouldn't now. Once she'd married Felix, served out the five years, she'd divorce him so he was free to escape her and she'd live out her life in happy solitude.

The dullness in her stomach was probably hunger. Those chips at the bar had looked amazing. "What does your dream wedding look like?" she asked. The question popped out before she'd filtered the words.

His chuckle was delicious, and right back in line with his version of normal. Maybe she'd imagined his disappointment? "I can't say I've spent any time sitting around considering it. Not what my brother had—something smaller and intimate. You?"

"I've never thought of it either. Until I found out about the money and the marriage stipulation, I'd never considered marriage."

"Never?"

"No. It's not an institution I wholly believe in. I know it works for some ... but not for me."

"Guess it's good I know your feelings on the subject now. Might you care to enlighten me as to why you feel it's not for you?"

"Just what I've told you before. My parents. My mum cheats constantly. She rules my father's life. He is oblivious and is besotted with her. He hasn't a clue that he's married to such a woman. How can two people be married and not know each other? It just ... it's turned me off the idea."

"I can see now why Henrik seemed a good choice. You two have been friends a long time. You knew the stakes."

"Yes, and having known him that long, I knew I'd never fall for him. I wouldn't have been putting myself in a position of being hurt."

"And with me?" he said into the darkness.

With him she was all too aware she was in a position to get hurt. But did she admit that to him? Would that be giving him too much power over her? Or was she overthinking the situation?

They'd nearly reached the car. Lights from the pub still blazed. The dim constant noise could be heard coming from inside but outside they were the only people about.

He stopped, sliding her to the ground and then turned to her, taking both her hands. "How do you feel about marriage and me? Am I a threat to your heart?"

She swallowed. Then nodded a quick, sharp nod.

"Then I guess we're in good company, because you are definitely a threat to mine."

Breathing was difficult. Why had breathing become difficult?

His hand nudged her the last few steps to the car. He opened the door, ushering her inside. She didn't dare look at his face.

Why had she just admitted that?

***

Felix had to stop himself from high-fiving the air. He was making progress with Sophia. Slowly, with every day, he beat down her walls a little more.

There was a long way to go until she trusted him implicitly, but he'd get there. Sophia deserved someone who loved her wholeheartedly, and Felix planned to be that man.

He slid into the car, noting that Sophia was avoiding his eyes—retreating slightly after having taken a step forwards. He held in an internal sigh. *Two steps forward, one step back.*

"Should we drive for a bit and see if we can find somewhere to stay?" he asked.

"There was a bed and breakfast as we were driving into Donegal. Let's try there."

"Your wish is my command."

He swung the car out onto the road, following the directions Sophia had keyed into satnav.

"Don't you have to get back home as soon as possible? You said Henrik knows where you are but your schedules are normally insane. You can't just disappear for days."

"I'll call George in the morning. I'll need him to organise a few things either way. Stefan was helping Henrik put out any fires in the interim. We're here now. Why not take a few extra days and see Ireland?"

"Is that fair? I mean, Henrik has only just married Eva. I'm sure they don't want to be inundated at this time. I'm happy to just go straight to Stenaco and get this done."

Ouch. He gritted his teeth. Now was not the time to push. He'd made progress. Time to just let the dust settle.

Later that night, Felix lay in the comfortable queen-sized bed. Alone.

The bed and breakfast had multiple rooms free, more was the pity, and it was probably for the best. Ever since Sophia had admitted she found Felix a threat to her heart, she'd folded back into her shell.

He flicked through messages on his phone, ignoring those from his assistant and zeroing in on one from Eva.

'When are you coming back to Stenaco?'

Felix frowned at the text. This wasn't something he could ignore. He tapped out a quick response.

'Probably tomorrow or the day afterwards. Why?'

Little dots immediately appeared on his screen before a new message popped up.

'Izzie has split to the Greek Islands with friends. Your father is livid. Henrik is swamped. I know you're helping Sophia but is

there any way we can speed up the process? You're needed back here.'

Dammit. What the devil was Izzie doing flitting off on holidays? He checked his thoughts. That didn't seem fair. He'd done his own share of skirting duties and lumping them on others so he could go off on spur-of-the-moment trips. If they needed him home then he and Sophia would return tomorrow. He hit reply.

'We'll fly back tomorrow. I'll call George in the morning to arrange flights. Any chance you could make Sophia the wedding dress of her dreams?'

The moment his phone rang he hit the decline button.

Better he check with Sophia before he spilled the beans completely to Eva about their trip. His phone buzzed again, this time with a call from Henrik. He declined that too, switching off his phone. He might be learning to be a little more responsible, but he didn't want to go changing his ways completely. Where would the fun in that be?

The plane touched down with a slight bump before it taxied along the tarmac and came to a smooth stop. The drive back to Belfast had been carried out in companionable silence, followed by the relatively painless four-hour flight. Felix had left Sophia well enough alone for which she was grateful.

She'd used that time to sort out logistical problems in her head such as where they'd get married, and how quickly they could gain the marriage licence and subsequent certificate for her to use as proof. There was an ache in her heart that had steadfastly refused to dissipate but she pushed it aside. The situation with her aunt was out of her control.

She could only hope that the other woman would approve of Sophia's decision to marry purely to obtain the money.

Except that's not the only reason you're marrying him.

She shrugged off the thought.

Felix took her hand as they departed the plane—the first time he'd touched her since she'd agreed to this madness.

Was he regretting his offer already?

A black SUV was waiting on the tarmac near the plane. Eva hopped out of the back, a mile-wide grin spreading across her face, her eyes zeroing straight in on Sophia's hand linked with Felix's. "Nice trip?" Eva asked, her eyes full of delight.

"I'll let Sophia fill you in." Felix squeezed her hand, then dropped it before hopping into the front passenger seat.

Her hand felt bereft the moment his left hers.

"Earth to Sophia?"

"Yes. Sorry. The trip was fine. How have things been here?"

Eva levelled her knowing gaze on Sophia before nodding her head at Felix's silhouette inside the car. "Deflecting, I see. You two looked rather cosy when you were walking off the plane before you spotted me."

"I ... we can talk about that later. I found my aunt. She's dead."

Eva's horrified gasp had her bodyguard spinning in their direction and taking two steps closer. Eva waved him away. "I'm so sorry." She enveloped Sophia in a hug, the warmth in the gesture bringing tears back to Sophia's eyes.

She'd spent half of the prior night crying. Her life was out of control. She'd never had a lot of control over it, thanks to her mother, but for some reason, finding out her unknown aunt had died before she'd even met her had really affected her mental balance.

Or is it because you've agreed to marry a man who jeopardises your carefully guarded heart and you're beyond scared?

"I never knew her. But it still hurts. Thank you."

"Come. Let's get you back to the palace. We can find ourselves a comforting pot of tea and talk."

"Tea sounds like heaven. Felix hates it. He drank it but I could see him practically gagging with every sip.

"That's a mighty personal observation. I can't wait to hear all about your trip."

Sophia held in a groan. Why had she said that about Felix? Though she supposed she'd have to tell Eva that they planned to marry. Wasn't like she'd be able to hold that news to herself forever. Both women hopped into the back of the SUV.

"How about you tell me what you and Henrik have been up too? Have you settled in okay now that the wedding is over?" Sophia asked.

"Don't think I'm missing the avoidance in your line of questioning. But as it happens, yes—very happily settled. We had the brunch, then more photos and press events, and dinners on top of dinners. I can't actually remember where we dined last night but Harriet was there. She was amazingly demure and friendly, which made me want to laugh but I acted cordial and pleasant in return and was very proud of myself. Don't want to spark anymore media storms —I've had enough of those for my lifetime."

"Harriet is a funny character. You're never really sure where you stand with her."

Felix piped up from the front seat. "Don't pay heed to anything Harriet says, Eva. She's always just happy to cause trouble. I think she finds it entertaining."

Sophia frowned. That was pretty harsh but unfortunately also true. Felix wasn't usually one to gossip so it surprised her that he'd do so about someone in their close circle, and to Eva, who was only a new part of the family.

Though Felix and Eva appeared to have kept a close friendship. Sophia was almost jealous of how easy they were around one another.

"Changing the subject back to what we were talking about earlier—I hear you're in need of a wedding dress?"

Sophia's head shot up, her gaze clashing with Felix's pained expression. "What?"

"Felix told me—never mind. I see I've really put my foot in something." Eva glanced between the two, throwing Felix a silent apology which Sophia didn't miss.

She sighed. "I guess it was only a matter of time before we had to tell people. Felix has agreed to step in and marry me so I can get my aunt's money. I was out of options."

"I do love to be a saviour, knight in shining armour and all that. You really just saved the best option until last." Felix showcased his teeth in a brilliant grin, his eyes pinning Sophia.

How did he always manage to turn her words around? It was clever, but also highly frustrating at times. Particularly those times when it put her on the spot.

"If you want to think that, so be it. Unfortunately though, Eva, Felix has jumped the gun in speaking to you. I do not, nor will I ever need, an actual wedding gown. I will be fine to wear something I already own. Wedding gowns are for real marriages."

Felix's eye's narrowed ever so slightly. "This will be a real marriage, lasting five years at least. More, if I have anything to say about it."

From the corner of her eye, Sophia caught Eva's mouth dropping open a little, like she was witnessing some poignant moment. Or perhaps a car crash. Sophia really needed to sit Felix down and have a word with him about what he could and couldn't share in public.

The car drove off towards the palace. She crossed her legs and leaned back in the seat, enjoying the familiar scenery out the window and hoping that her stance spoke of an end to their conversation. At least her part in it. She'd spent a lot of time in Stenaco, in particular the country's capital, Geravia. Her mother had certainly never had a problem with her coming and Sophia had always associated it with being able to finally breathe fresh air and escape.

Her mother had always encouraged her friendship with Henrik. Her hints that Sophia could end up with a title far greater than Lady had been as subtle as a sledgehammer. It was hard to know what Cynthia would make of the announcement of her upcoming marriage to Felix.

She'd become a princess, for a time at least.

She swallowed. Was she doing the right thing? Felix kept pushing, wanting this to be … something … but there was a part of her that just wouldn't trust his word. Why her? Why now?

Love was a fool's game. One she did not want to dabble in.

Except she'd just placed her piece on the game board.

10

"*D*o you want the good news or the bad news?"

Felix flicked his gaze up, watching his brother stride towards the desk where he sat. Ever since they'd arrived back at the palace, he'd pretty much been chained to this darn table, going through correspondence that George had gleefully dumped on him.

"I've always hated it when people ask me that. I only ever want good news."

"Tough biscuits. I only have bad."

Henrik sat, managing to look relaxed yet regal at the same time. By comparison, Felix slouched back in his chair and crossed his socked feet on the corner of his desk. "I believe the term you're looking for there was 'tough cookie' but let's not get sidetracked. You appear to be almost as gleeful as George was to deliver this 'bad news'. Have at it, then?"

"Sophia's mother is attending the ball Friday night."

Felix bounded up to a straight position. "Please tell me you're joking."

"I'm not really known for joking."

"No, you're right. That's a mighty big shame."

"Lady Cynthia coming to the ball or my lack of humour?"

The brothers looked at each other, then Henrik shrugged.

"Both," Felix replied with Henrik simultaneously.

Lady Cynthia was the last person he wanted around right now. Sophia was already skittish since they'd been ordered back. If Felix had his way, he'd sweep her right back to Ireland. They'd been forming a connection there. Sophia had been different; she'd allowed him in. Only a tiny bit, but it had happened. Enough to give him hope that he wasn't running a fool's race. "Definitely no good news?"

The corner of Henrik's mouth twitched. "I'm gifting you a fancy dinner out tomorrow night. Does that count?"

Felix narrowed his gaze. "Depends. Who is it with?"

"The museum board. And Izzie."

"I thought she was in Greece?"

"She is. But that's now also your problem. Don't say I never give you anything."

Felix just shook his head. He owed Henrik. Having skipped away straight after his brother's wedding was pretty low when he should have been stepping up to take on more responsibility, giving Henrik and Eva some time to adjust to married life.

Now he *really* wished he could have stayed in Ireland.

"You'll do it?" Henrik asked, his tone indicating that no wasn't an option.

"Couldn't think of anything I'd rather do."

"Then you need to get out more. Speaking of getting out, how was Ireland? Eva said you and Sophia hit a road block that's resulted in wedding bells. Congratulations. I hope I don't have to add that if you hurt my friend, brother or not, I'll have to hurt you."

"I'd like to see you try. But either way, you're safe. If anyone is going to be hurt it will be me. Sophia seems a little immune to romance and love."

"You've never backed down from a challenge. If this is real, you won't back down from this either."

"No. I won't. But for the first time in my life, I'm also not sure I'll win. I hadn't realised how bad her home situation was."

Henrik gave Felix a sharp look. "What do you mean? I know she doesn't get along with her mother."

"Doesn't get along with her? It's a hell of a lot more than that! The woman runs Sophia's life like a dictator. She's got Sophia trapped. She can't be honest with her father, tell him the truth about Cynthia's cheating, which is eating her up inside because if she does, Cynthia will ruin her charity."

Henrik sat back in his seat. "I didn't know."

"But haven't you been helping her?"

"I've loaned her some money a few times. She mentioned her mum goes through her accounts and there were things she didn't want her to see. I wasn't aware she was being held hostage in an emotional and financial sense." Henrik's mouth thinned.

Felix hadn't meant to tell his brother everything. Part of him had assumed that Sophia had shared those details with him already. That she'd chosen to share them with him first gave him a little bright spark of hope. "Send me the details and I'll do what I can for tomorrow night."

"Is that your polite way of dismissing me?"

"I wasn't trying to be polite." Felix shrugged, his lips twitching.

Henrik stood and started walking towards the door

before he stopped and glanced back over his shoulder. "So is there a wedding date?"

Felix shook his head. His lawyer hadn't called him back yet. If he had his way, he'd be dragging Sophia off to the registry at their earliest convenience. But things weren't going his way. He'd just have to wait and hope that the extra time didn't end with Sophia changing her mind.

She might want a marriage of convenience but he had every intention of making it a marriage of love.

Sophia took a sip of her hot tea, the milky, sweet liquid slipping down her throat and soothing her nerves immediately. Eva had been called away to take a phone call, leaving Sophia alone. The momentary reprieve from any questions or scrutiny was welcome.

Not that Eva didn't have good intentions, but since arriving back in Stenaco, Sophia's worries over her decision had skyrocketed.

The news that her mother would be arriving the day after tomorrow hadn't helped. She'd been hoping to not have to see her again until she could impart the information that she had found a way to free herself from her mother's clutches. That she would no longer be used as a pawn in her mother's twisted game.

She didn't blame the palace for inviting Lady Cynthia. After the media mix-up and rumours about Eva being involved with both brothers, plus Sophia's own supposed pending engagement to Henrik, it made sense that the palace wanted to do damage control. Sophia and her family had been encouraged to attend as many events as possible to show a happy front.

But there was no getting away from the ball at the end of the week. Her mother would be there, and unless Felix worked a miracle, she wouldn't have time to marry and secure her money before then.

"What's that face about?" Eva asked, resuming her seat at the alfresco table.

"My mother."

"I'm so sorry about the ball. I know you'd prefer she wasn't invited but our press officer insisted and—"

"No, please don't apologise. It makes sense. I certainly don't want to do anything that would rock the boat. The situation is only just stabilising. I just wish I could have waited to see my mother until I'd secured my freedom."

"I'm positive Felix has already offered … but if this is just a matter of money, let us help you? I know Henrik wouldn't hesitate to say yes."

"Felix has already offered. It's not just the money. I mean, obviously a lot of it is the money—that's the key—but I don't want to have to borrow it from someone else to achieve my freedom. I'll just feel indebted to them. I want to be able to do this by myself. Does that make any kind of rational sense?"

Eva cocked her head to the side, then nodded. "Yes. I understand."

Felix swept out onto the balcony, his frown clearing the moment his eyes found Sophia's. "Hello, my beautiful bride-to-be."

Sophia tried not to let the pleasure at those words show. This wasn't a love match. This wasn't even a relationship match. She swallowed, feeling like she was being sucked into a vortex of her thoughts. Was she really ready to marry a man she'd never even been on a date with?

"Try not to let that absolute delight show. You'll make

my ego explode." Felix still held a smile but his eyes held concern. "Sorry for practically disappearing yesterday. George has taken great pleasure in burying me in paperwork."

"Payback for disappearing for a few days without telling anyone perhaps?" Eva said.

"I told people. I told you and Henrik."

"You also asked us not to share your location. George was just put out you didn't think of him, since he considers himself your right-hand man. Any luck with Izzie?"

"Not exactly. She screened my calls. I talked a mate into calling but the moment he suggested she needed to phone home she hung up on him, no doubt twigging that I'd requested the call."

"The king won't be pleased. I think he was counting on your influence to get her to come home. There have been many heated discussions between them."

"Izzie's been a bit funny of late. I'll track her down. Pushing her to do something she doesn't want to won't result in her coming home. It will only make her run faster."

"Sounds like a family trait."

"Alas, it leaves me without a date for the board dinner tonight. Would you care to join me, sweet Sophia?"

"Not if you're going to call me that again."

"I'll work on a better name. So?"

"Okay."

"You know how to make a guy feel special. I'll leave you ladies to your tea. Dinner is at seven. I'll come collect you from your room at six."

He meandered back inside, whistling a cheery tune.

"Sophia, what is going on? I had thought when Felix mentioned wedding bells that you two had become an item?"

"No. Well. He wants us to be."

"But you're not interested?"

"Unfortunately the opposite. I am interested. But I don't want to be. Felix makes me feel things I've never felt before. He threatens my balance. We've gone from knowing each other for years, and don't get me wrong, I've always found him ... attractive ... in a way I shouldn't have, but I've never thought he'd paid me the slightest bit of notice. Now I find out I'm the reason he came looking for you, and that he's always had feelings for me, and wants to try a relationship, and I'm just supposed to accept that? All I can think is that he's dated half of Europe. Why me? And why now?"

"You don't trust his word."

"No. And I don't know how I ever will."

"But you'll marry him?"

Sophia felt like she was tearing apart. "It's an impossible situation, I know."

"Can I ask a favour?" Sophia looked at her friend, then gave a simple nod. "Don't just write Felix off. I know he's had a reputation, but there's more there than you're seeing. He's a good guy."

Sophia nodded again, not trusting her voice. He was a good guy. But was it enough?

Was she enough?

11

The ballroom was filled with people dripping in riches. Sophia had been to many events just like this one, but never had she felt this level of nerves. Felix stood close beside her, his body heat providing a sensory sort of comfort. She hadn't had much time these past three days to discuss anything with him regarding their upcoming marriage. The Museum board dinner had been the last time they'd been alone and that had been filled with constant interruptions—not the ideal setting to chat wedding specifics. At least that's what Sophia had reasoned with herself afterwards.

The paperwork still wasn't finalised. Felix knew time was not on her side and she could only trust that he was doing everything he could to arrange it.

There was that word again. *Trust.*

"You look ravishing," Felix whispered at her ear. "Pale icy blue is really your colour."

Sophia glanced at her gown. Her mother had sent it over with a demand she wear it. Apparently it was part of a new couture collection being shown next week. Points to Cynthia

—she'd pulled out all the stops for this one. Sophia was partly scared and partly curious to see what her mother would be wearing if she'd sent this to her. She was out to make a splash.

The dress glittered with crystals. The full satin skirts ballooned out around her. It made her feel a little like Cinderella, though that was a totally idiotic and fanciful thought.

Besides, glass slippers would have to be seriously uncomfortable. She kicked out the hem of her skirts, revealing the almond shape of her Louboutin heels, the fronts covered in Swarovski crystals. At least she knew every cent paid for both of these items went to workers under good conditions.

"You're being very quiet though. People are going to talk."

Sophia readjusted her mind. Felix was right; she needed to get out of her head. "Sorry. Thank you for the compliment. I'm waiting for my mother to arrive. It's put me on edge."

"Understandably. Are you going to tell her?"

"About our agreement?"

"Let's call it an engagement—far nicer."

"I'd prefer not to tell her, if it's all the same. She can come to her own conclusions about seeing us together but until we have that marriage certificate and it's with my aunt's lawyer, I'd really appreciate keeping our news to ourselves."

"As you wish."

Sophia sensed her mother's presence. It was like an oppressive force bearing down on her, one that left a wake of Dior wafting behind her.

"Darling, *so* good to see you. You've been missed in London. The dress suits you, though it would have looked better with your hair done differently." She placed a kiss against Sophia's cheek, her cold hands gripping Sophia's upper arms.

"Mother. Lovely of you to come all of this way. Is Dad here?"

"No. He had something with the polo club. He sends his love."

Sophia gritted her teeth underneath her smile. She'd put money on the fact that her mother had arranged whatever polo thing was on so she didn't have to bring her husband.

Cynthia turned her attention from Sophia to the man beside her. "Prince Felix, it's always a pleasure to see you," she all but purred. The sound grated on Sophia. How did people not see how fake her mother was?

"Lady Cynthia. It is our pleasure to have you visit our little country."

George walked over, offering a short bow before he interrupted. "Excuse me, Prince Felix. There is a phone call for you."

Felix flicked his gaze to Sophia. "I'll return the call tomorrow please, George."

"I'm afraid it's urgent. It's Princess Isabella."

Felix muttered something unintelligible under his breath. She dropped her hand to brush gently against his, offering a small nod.

She hoped he'd understand her gesture. He looked at her fingers, letting out a small sigh, then glanced back to George.

"Please excuse me, ladies." His mouth was set.

Sophia couldn't help but feel a little helpless being left standing with her mother. Even in a crowded room she didn't feel safe from criticism.

"The dress does look good. I hope you appreciate my sending it over. It would have been a travesty for you to have worn something a second time or, heaven forbid, something of your friend's."

"How was Dad before you left?"

Cynthia threw her a cutting look. "Don't start, Sophia. Remember, I hold the upper hand. One of your friends called the house—apparently some news about a factory?"

Sophia's heart skipped. What factory? Why had they called? She'd been so caught up in her own problems, she'd barely checked in with her friends at the charity. She looked about the room. The evening had only just started. It wouldn't be appropriate for her to skip off yet. Even if she desperately wanted to. She held in a sigh, instead feigning an interest in her nails.

Her mother leant in close, her voice sharp but low. "Why weren't you at the brunch?"

So they were back to this. Did they really have to rehash old subjects?

"I told you. I wasn't feeling well."

"And Prince Felix? Don't think I'm blind. I saw you touch his hand just now. Are you two a thing?"

"So what if we are? It's no business of yours who I'm seeing."

"Don't be so stupid. He'll make you a laughing stock. I honestly don't know why you keep bothering to come here. Your chance with Henrik is gone. Felix won't commit to you. He won't ever marry unless his father makes it an official order and I can't see the old man doing that now that Henrik's married. The pressure has been relieved."

"Old man? You do know King Bastian is a year younger than you."

If looks could kill. Sophia probably shouldn't have said

that, but she couldn't help it. Hurt and rage spun through her body like pounding waves. Her mother had never understood the bond that Sophia felt to the Stenish royal family. Mainly because she didn't have a maternal bone in her body.

"You will have breakfast with me in the morning and then we will fly home together. I can only assume your friend's call means you'll be looking for more money for that little charity of yours. If you want it, you'll be waiting to leave with me tomorrow."

Cynthia spun on her heel, the move flouncing the many layers of her skirt into Sophia. She bit her tongue, holding back the denial. Her mother was walking away. Refusal at this stage would only call her back and all Sophia wanted to do was leave—in any direction opposite her mothers. Not that it appeared that would be an option.

Sophia gulped in a deep breath of air, letting it out as slowly as possible, hoping to calm her beating heart. Her mother just made her so mad these days. When she'd been younger, she'd basked in the attention from her, lapping up the endless stream of beautiful clothing, expensive shoes, and designer handbags. She'd talked to anyone she was directed to, said what she was told. As she grew older, pleasing her mother had become harder. The criticism had started to take over the praise. Nothing she did seemed right. At twenty-five, Sophia had decided she'd had enough. She'd told her mother she wanted to move out of the family home. It had been time for her to think about what she wanted to do with her life.

How naive she'd been. *How stupid.* The very words said to her by her mother. What did she think she'd do about money? It didn't grow on trees, and Sophia wasn't employable.

Those words had hurt. Mainly as they were the truth. Sophia hated herself for not just walking out then. She could have found an entry-level job. She'd known a lot of people. That had been her chance to change but she hadn't taken it. Because she'd been too scared.

"Lady Sophia, I presume?"

Sophia turned towards the voice. A slim brunette in a skintight beaded maroon dress met her gaze. The other woman was striking, her brown eyes surrounded by heavy make-up that made her appear seductive but did nothing to detract from her perfect curvy figure.

Sophia held in a sigh tinged with jealousy. "Yes. You are?" She tilted her chin up a little, taking satisfaction that she was taller than this woman. For some reason this woman rubbed her the wrong way. Or was that just residual annoyance from her encounter with her mother?

"Charlotte. I'm Harriet's cousin."

Her eyes flicked over the other woman's shoulder, catching Harriet staring at them.

"Pleasure to meet you. Should we go see your cousin? I don't believe I've said hello to her tonight yet." Nor had she particularly wanted to but it would be rude not to now she'd caught her gaze.

"You can do that later. I wanted to give you a friendly warning."

"Excuse me?"

"About Prince Felix."

She froze at those words, her face still a serene mask but underneath she'd become as scattered as rose petals at a wedding. Instead of speaking, she raised a single brow.

"He told you he hasn't been with anyone for months, right?"

How the hell did this woman know that? Had Felix told her? Why would that come up in conversation?

Apparently her silence was enough for the other woman to continue.

"He was lying. He and I had a weekend together a month ago. After an event here."

With every word spoken, Sophia's throat closed over. Her hands clenched, her nails digging in, but she forced herself to relax them. Outward calm was the key. Never let them see your pain. Never let them see they were getting to you. "How wonderful for you. I don't see how it is relevant though." Her smile was fake, but as the other woman's eyes narrowed with fury, it became a little more genuine.

Instead of hanging around to see what she'd say next, Sophia turned and walked away.

Felix had looked her in the eye and sworn he'd not been with anyone else. She'd promised to try and trust him. That was their agreement. Their time in Ireland had shown her a new side to Felix, one that she struggled to hold back from. All that time he'd been running around as a playboy it had been easy to dismiss him. But with his full attention on her? With his continual efforts to prove he'd changed? Not once had he tried to just take her to bed. And it wasn't like she hadn't offered.

No.

She needed to give Felix the benefit of the doubt. She'd just ask him. That couldn't be that hard, right?

Plus there were more important things in the world than squabbling with another socialite who just appeared to be out to make trouble. She needed to find out why her friend had contacted her and how she could help with this factory news.

And she still had to get married.

Felix mentally cursed for what seemed the seventh time. "Izzie, you need to come home. I understand you need space, but now isn't the time. You know what the schedule is like now Henrik and Eva are married. They are about to embark on a tour around the country. You and I must be here."

"Says you, who gallivanted off to Northern Ireland on a whim." Izzie's tone was dry.

"Wait, how'd you know where I went?"

"Never mind that. Tell Dad if he wants me to come home, he can call and apologise."

"For what?" Felix was getting frustrated. Their phone call had been going in a circle and he wanted to get back to Sophia to make sure she was coping okay. Now he understood the full situation with her mother, he felt an added level of ... protectiveness.

"He knows," Izzie deadpanned.

"Are you really going to just dump me in the middle of this?"

"You called me, kitty-kat," she sing-songed.

Was she drunk? A concerning thought since it was only an hour later in Greece than it was here. He opened his mouth to beg one last time for her to just see sense but was met by the *beep, beep* of a disconnected call.

Dammit.

That problem would have to be shelved. He needed to get back to Sophia.

Walking with clipped footsteps down the polished corridor towards the ballroom, he almost collided with the woman in question.

"Woah. You okay? You look a million miles away."

Her brisk steps were brought up short. "Felix! You surprised me."

"Escaping already? Or did you miss me so much you had to come find me?"

She rolled her eyes. As he'd hoped, but at least it had put a little more colour back in her cheeks. She looked ... worried.

"Do you know Harriet's cousin?"

Her question threw him. "Charlotte? Yes. I've met her a few times. Is she here?"

"Yes. Have you seen her recently?" Sophia's eyes darted away from his.

What was this about? He narrowed his gaze at Sophia, pinning her to the spot. "Last month. For the musea opening gala. Where has that pretty head of yours gone?"

Hurt flashed in her eyes at his words but she blinked it quickly away. "Nowhere. Never mind. I was just curious."

"What did she say?"

"Nothing."

"You're protesting too much."

"Can I use your office to make a phone call?"

As a segue to distract him, he had to say it worked well. He filed the information in the back of his mind to find out what Charlotte or whoever had said. It certainly hadn't been "nothing" as Sophia claimed.

"Of course. I'll take you."

"Oh, no. You don't need to. You're needed inside."

"I'll take you," he repeated, sliding his arm about her waist and walking them down the corridor.

He drank in her scent, the fresh, floral notes bringing new energy to his body.

Her heels brought her almost in line with his eyes. His

nose was level with her ear and he ached to bend slightly and place a kiss against the delicate skin behind it.

She shivered, like she'd sensed his thoughts.

The doors to the balcony at the end of the hall were open, moonlight spilling through. The candle ahead that indicated his office door flickered in the slight breeze. He ached to draw Sophia out into the evening air and put his thoughts into actions, to help her forget her worries but she'd asked to use his office.

"How did things go with your mother?"

"About as well as expected. She warned me off you. Apparently noticed we were cosy."

"Doesn't she want you to marry a prince anymore?"

"You're not the marrying or commitment type, according to her."

Felix ground his teeth to stop his immediate response. *Pot. Kettle. Black. Much?* "What did you say to that?" he asked.

"Nothing. With my mother, I've learned the least said, the better."

Felix stilled their walk, turning her to face him. "Do *you* believe her?"

She paused, appearing to choose her words carefully. She had tiny frown lines between her brows and he stroked a thumb down the smooth skin, unable to stop himself.

"If you'd asked me at Henrik's wedding, I'd have said yes." Her words were soft. Hypnotic.

"And now?"

"Now ... I believe that you *want* to be the marrying and commitment type."

Her choice of words were astute. She hadn't said she believed him. Just that she thought he believed it. It was a slight word difference but spoke volumes. He still had a way to go. "It's a step in the right direction. I'll wear you down, Sophia, even if it takes a lifetime."

A soft gasp left those delicious lips of hers. He bent his head slightly, nuzzling his nose to hers, his eyes linking with hers. Questioning. Begging.

Her eyes fluttered shut as she leaned in, her breath as wispy as lace against his lips before they met his in a soft kiss. He kept his eyes open, enjoying the movement dance behind her lids. He ran his tongue along her bottom lip, tasting just her. Her soft sigh brought him undone. He sank into the kiss, unable to keep his eyes open. He slipped into a sort of heaven created only when her lips met his. How often did he dream of her mouth? Ever more so now that he'd experienced it first-hand.

She was addictive. Kissing her was fast becoming his everything. It had never felt like this before—like he was totally, one hundred per cent invested. This time, his heart was right there with him and it took any intimacy with her to the next level.

He stepped closer, bringing her body into delicious contact with his, his arms snaking around her waist to hold her against him. She moaned, the sound vibrating through his chest. He ached to undo every last tiny button down the back of her dress and reveal her naked form. To be able to kiss every inch of her silken skin. How had he lived life without knowing this fine pleasure? How had he held himself back from her so long?

He'd never forget the pleasure of her in his arms.

His fingers clenched then relaxed against her slim figure. He needed to take stop this before he lost his mind. His lips parted from hers, stealing one more tiny nip before he took a physical step back. One tiny embrace and she'd sent him up in flames.

"You make my head spin when you do that," Sophia said breathlessly.

Felix could say the same thing about her. "I should do it more often then."

"You'll have me walking into doors and walls."

"I'd stop you. C'mon. Let's get you to my office so you can make your call before you send me any further down this salacious path."

"Excuse me. That kiss was all you."

"No way, honey. It was both of us. You have to admit, there's a certain new level of electricity that sparks when we kiss. I've never felt that with anyone else." He didn't know why he'd admitted that but Sophia's body relaxed against his, as if the words were spreading throughout her whole body. Her face shone, her smile spreading wide at his words.

She cocked her head to the side, her brows quirking a little. "I know you said before that you wanted us to get to know each other better, but I think we're past that now. Why haven't you taken me to bed?"

Felix choked. "Uh, well. Is that an invitation?"

"Do you need one?"

He sucked in air. He got the feeling his answer here would mean a lot. He didn't want to screw it up. "I do want an invitation, yes. But more than that, I want you to be sure. I *know* I'm sure. I know we'll be good together. One kiss is enough to tell me that. Trust me when I say not making love to you is driving me insane. Blue balls has taken on a new meaning. But I want you to know this is more than that for me. I want you in bed, yes. But I also want to be in here ..." he tapped her head, "... and most importantly, I want to be in here." He tapped her heart.

He left his finger on her chest a moment before sliding it

across and between her breasts. After hitting the silk band at her waist, he dropped his hand.

She stared at him with a helpless sort of wonder. Her mouth had slipped open, her eyes wide. Those icy-blue depths were swirling. They held a silvery glint in them that almost glowed in the darkened corridor. "You're serious, aren't you?" she said, part question, part statement.

"I've never been more serious in my life."

12

Sophia hung up the phone. Her gaze swung around Felix's office, taking in the neat yet elegant space. She really needed to get back to London to deal with some work. Her friend Rachel had been trying to cover most of the overflow but it was time for her to step in and do something. As nice as her trip here and to Ireland had been, she couldn't just sit around and wait for Felix to come up with the paperwork.

Her finger touched her lips, prodding at the soft skin still tingling from the feel of his mouth against hers. In fact, all of her still tingled with delicious anticipation.

Felix had gone above and beyond during their time in Ireland. Her reaction to Charlotte's words, and her believing Felix's response ... didn't that tell her something? Didn't that tell her she was fighting a battle that maybe she should just be embracing?

He'd said he was ready to commit to her. Obviously normal circumstances would dictate they start with dating, not marriage ... but this marriage would give her everything she'd wanted. And possibly a man she'd never thought she should.

She ached to have him here, back beside her, for it to just be the two of them again.

If she defied her mother tomorrow, that would take away her last obstacle. Or was she her own obstacle? Sophia smiled, warmth spreading through her at the idea of cheating her mother of her demands and finally committing to Felix.

She stood, collecting up the skirts of her dress so she didn't trip on them, and walked out of the room and was brought up short. Felix was leaning against the corridor wall, head bent, hands laced behind his back. She must have made a noise as his head turned to her, his eyes locking with hers, deepening with desire. His gaze travelled down to her toes and back up. "You really do look beautiful."

"Are you one hundred per cent certain about marrying me?"

He frowned. "Interesting response to a compliment, but yes, I've never been more certain in my life. In fact, that's why I've stayed. George just delivered the good news: he has our marriage licence."

"Then let's go."

"Go?"

"Get married."

"Right now?"

"Yes. I don't want to wait. I don't want to go back to London with my mother tomorrow and I don't want to live under the same roof as her ever again.I can't stomach another moment of her presence knowing that I have this option. I have one week left to meet the stipulations so let's go get married. Then I can courier the marriage certificate to the lawyer in Ireland and I'm free."

"I can't—okay."

"No, stop. What were you going to say?"

"I can't believe I'm saying this, but the registry's will be closed, and I've promised Henrik I'll help him first thing. I can call and have a registry opened—"

"No." She stepped closer, holding her hand up to still his movement. "It's late. We're meant to be at the ball. It can wait until tomorrow afternoon."

"But you said your mother told you to be on a plane tomorrow."

Sophia sucked in a deep breath. Her knees wobbled a little but she hoped the dress would hide that. As much as she wanted to dive in head first now that she'd made her mind up she refused to become her mother and just make demands, expecting they be answered. Besides, Felix had only just come back from helping her, he had commitments here and it wasn't fair for him to drop all of those to marry her just because she'd had a sudden moment of clarity. She'd rearrange her plans a little. She could afford a few more days. Felix had done so much already to make this happen.

"She did, and I'll go. I was getting ahead of myself. I need to see my friend in London, pack up some clothes, find something to wear. Then I can meet you back here to get married. I presume you want to marry in Stenaco?"

His chest expanded, his eyes widening like he couldn't believe everything that was coming out of her mouth. "It doesn't have to be here. Is it easier for me to come to London to meet you?"

She laughed. "It would save me trying to sort out a plane fare. Are you okay with that?"

"You pack a bag, and I'll organise everything else." He

pushed away from the wall and walked with purpose towards her. He stopped a hair's breadth away, his hands circling her waist as his head dipped to hers. He swept her back over his arm, dipping her low as he captured her waiting lips in what could only be described as a Hollywood kiss. He was every taste of heaven, freedom, and all the things she'd never thought she wanted nor needed. Euphoria spread around her torso, every nerve point springing into action, every vein pumping blood with excessive force. All of her was alive with want for this man.

His mouth shifted, kissing and sucking his way to the side of her neck. He moaned behind her ear and the vibration nearly sent her spinning into a world of stars. Why had she been holding him at arm's length? Hadn't he shown he was committed to her? She wanted him; he wanted her. This, at least, was simple.

"I want you," she whispered. "I don't want to wait any longer."

She wanted to say she believed him wholeheartedly. That she trusted him implicitly. But one tiny speck in her held back.

Felix's kisses paused for a millisecond before they resumed with gusto, his lips trailing towards the top of her dress. She dropped her head back, the move dislodging the small tiara that had been placed there. The clatter of it hitting polished wooden floors paused his progress.

He pulled Sophia back to a standing position, then bent to collect the darn thing. "It seems I've dislodged your halo."

She giggled, unable to stop the tinkling sound erupting. Her whole body was alive with delight and wonder and exhilaration at the thought of what was to come. "I'm pretty sure it's not a halo."

"It shines on your head like one. Do you really want this? Because now would be the time to break it to me. Once I take you to my room, I can't promise I'll be able to stop. Though I guess I could try a bath filled with ice—"

She put a finger to his lips. He immediately kissed it with a feather-light touch. "I'm sure. Don't make me beg."

"If anyone will be begging, I'm pretty sure it's going to be me." He leaned in and kissed her nose, then her forehead, and then pressed the lightest of kisses against her mouth. "Come with me, my fiancée."

His movements were gentle, but the look in his eyes told her she shouldn't expect to get much sleep that night.

Which was just as well, as that was exactly what she was hoping for.

Felix rolled over in bed, instinctively sensing that Sophia was already gone before he ran his palm across the cool sheets. His body burned with memories of last night, of having her pliant and wanton in his arms. He'd tried to hold back his enthusiasm but he needn't have worried. Sophia had met him every step of the way. Every kiss, every touch had been welcomed with equal amounts of desire and need.

He'd felt complete when she'd been in his arms.

Words of love had almost slipped past his lips but he'd called them back. It could wait until the timing was just perfect. He wanted his ring on her finger, her name intrinsically linked to his in matrimony. He didn't want any doubt in her mind around his actions when he laid his soul bare.

She'd mentioned something about having to pander to her mother over breakfast. Rolling to his other side, a short glance at his clock told him it was after nine and he'd slept in. Amazing that no one had come in and shooed him out of bed for duties.

He lay on his back, staring at the ceiling. How often in the past few months had he stared at this view, wishing that he could be sharing it with Sophia? He'd made the assumption that she'd move into the palace here with him, but perhaps that was too hasty. Would she even want to live in his country?

It dawned on him that they hadn't sat down and discussed any of the specifics of this marriage. His focus had solely been on showing her he was committed to doing this for her, that he wanted her regardless of how that looked. Given her relationship with her mother, he couldn't see her opting to stay at her home in London. Whilst he knew she'd developed feelings for him, her main goal still appeared to be freedom from Cynthia.

Well, maybe he'd just have to shift her focus a little.

She didn't want a big wedding, but that didn't mean she didn't want a proper wedding. One with a couture gown, elegant flowers, and the proverbial glass slippers. And he had just the woman, make that two women, who could help.

Surely this would also bring Izzie back from whatever hole she was hiding out in—a fact that could only prove to be a bonus.

Flipping the sheets back, he waltzed naked across the room, heading for his en suite.

A knock sounded before his brother Henrik walked into the room. "Good God, man, you need to put a warning sign up if you're going to walk around flinging that thing about the place."

"Right. Like you don't enjoy waltzing about naked every morning sporting a semi?"

"If I have time to spare whilst naked, I can assure you,

I'm putting my body to better use. And I don't mean walking."

"I don't need visuals, thanks. It was bad enough having to kiss your wife to get you to come to your senses."

"Yeah, yeah. Keep telling yourself that. I saw Sophia this morning out on the terrace with her mother. She looked ... distracted."

"Pleasant dreams, I believe."

"So you two ...?" Henrik raised a brow, a cheeky grin in place.

"We're getting married. Day after tomorrow, in London."

"Congratulations. I'd say that's fast but I get there are circumstances. Has she told you everything?"

"I think so. I feel like we shared a lot whilst we were in Ireland. Connected in a way that was emotional, instead of just physical."

"I'm impressed. You're a new man."

"I do believe you're correct, brother. So? You guys can shirk duties to make the wedding, right? It wouldn't be the same if you weren't there."

"Wouldn't miss it for anything. I never thought I'd see the day."

Felix laughed, slapping his brother on the shoulder. A naked hug just seemed too wrong, even if he was completely comfortable in this state.

Most people would be shocked when news broke that he'd committed to someone. There'd be sceptics, and things would be said. But he didn't care. He'd always believed deep down that he'd find his way there eventually. He'd just taken an incredibly scenic route to make sure.

Couldn't fault a guy for that.

"You want me to design and make you a wedding dress in less than twenty-four hours?" Eva fell into a chair, laughing and clutching her stomach. "You're hilarious, brother."

"I'm not joking. If it's too much, I need you to find me my second-best option."

Eva wiped tears from the corner of her eye. "I'm not a miracle worker!"

"You turned my brother back into a human being. Let me assure you, you're exactly that."

Eva shook her head at him, disbelief replacing the humour from moments ago. "Okay. I may have started something after your message from a few days ago. But it's going to take work. And you're going to owe me. Big time. Like, naming your first-born after me."

"What if it's a boy?"

"Evan would be sufficient."

"Deal."

"I'll give you a list of all the other things it's going to take but that can wait. You know Izzie needs to be there too?"

"On it. She's my next stop."

"I feel privileged you came to me first." She held out her cheek for him to peck.

"You're more local than she is." He rolled his eyes, not mentioning that getting Eva to design and make a couture gown was the lesser of the two tasks. Talking Izzie into anything she didn't want to do was hard work. He sensed that part of her being disgruntled had to do with the family dynamics. He just didn't know how to broach that topic without sending her tumbling farther away.

"Sit up straight, darling. Just because we're on a plane doesn't mean your deportment isn't important."

Sophia straightened. She couldn't even be sure if the voice came from outside her head or inside it as well. Just being in her mother's presence was changing her, like she'd been breathing fresh air and now the sheet had been pulled back over head. Her mother sat beside her, legs demurely crossed in her spacious seat, sipping at ice-cold champagne. She was certain it was arctic in temperature since her mother had sent their first two glasses back, requesting they make them colder.

Sophia had tried to catch the flight attendant's eye to offer a silent apology but the poor man hadn't so much as looked up.

"There's a dinner function tonight at Silvio's. I need you to speak with a man named Garry Silvestri."

"Why?"

Cynthia threw her a sharp look. "What do you mean why? Just talk to him, butter him up, delight him with your apparently fabulous conversation and beauty."

Don't say it, Sophia. You're on the home stretch—remember that.

Heeding her internal voice, she lifted her lips in a smile, though it didn't reach her eyes. But since her mother never bothered to keep her focus on Sophia for more than two seconds, it wouldn't matter. She could probably stick her tongue out, roll her eyes inwards, or do a puffer fish impersonation and she doubted it would be seen. Unless Cynthia was in a public place with people who mattered, she didn't bother to give her gaze to others.

Just her orders.

Sophia's phone vibrated against her thigh. Excusing

herself, she slipped into the tiny bathroom to read her message. No way did she want to risk any chance of her mother seeing her phone.

Felix.

Just seeing his name on the screen eased the tightness in her chest, eased the ache between her shoulders. How had she managed to cope for all of these years without having him there? Perhaps because she'd never allowed herself to depend on anyone else.

He'd found a place for the wedding, and he gave her a time and an address, signing the short message with regrets that he had woken to an empty bed. He missed her.

She missed him too. But she didn't type that back.

What they had felt ... complicated still. Like they were doing everything out of order. She had feelings invested. Felix had said he had feelings invested. But he hadn't come out and said the *L* word.

She swallowed.

Did she want him to?

Pushing the thought to the back of her mind, she re-pocketed the phone, jammed down the flush button, and returned to her seat.

The rest of the short flight was completed in almost silence. Sophia read the paperwork that her friend had emailed to her about the factory that was under suspicion of breaking rules around work conditions. It was always tricky when a new situation like this came about. She didn't want their work to shut the factory down—that would just result in more losses of jobs—she just wanted to offer support to ensure that everyone working there received a fair deal. They provided the funds to all the workers until the situation was fixed. That was how they operated.

It gave her hope that she was giving to those in need—giving kids a chance at growing up in a more stable environment, and hopefully added valuable time with their families.

All things she'd never had from her mother.

After the seamless trip from the airport into town, Sophia's mother waltzed into their Chelsea town house, barely flicking the doorman a glance, and proceeded straight to her office without a backwards look. Sophia let out the breath she'd been holding. *Back home.*

Now seemed as good a time as any to start stashing some of her clothes so she could make a quick getaway. Plus she needed to find an outfit to wear for her wedding.

Her lips wobbled a little at the thought.

"Sweetheart, how was the wedding?"

She jumped at her father's words before realisation hit that he was talking about Eva and Henrik's wedding—not her own pending nuptials.

He swept into the room and his warm arms enveloped her in a giant hug. She might not have missed being here, but she certainly missed her dad.

She pulled back slightly. "It was beautiful. Why are you at home? Isn't this your golf day?"

He shrugged, an odd look on his face. "Felt a bit crook, and wanted to be here for when you got back."

"Is something wrong?"

His face did look a little pale and stretched.

"Nothing you need to worry about. I'll leave you to unpack." He patted her shoulder and went to walk away before he turned. "I almost forgot—a delivery came for you about half an hour ago. I popped it on your bed."

Sophia frowned.

Walking into her spacious room, she spotted the

wrapped Harrods boxes on her bed immediately, topped with a square maroon velvet one sitting in pride of place.. She swallowed, a strange sensation taking over.

Her fingers trembled as she flipped the lid open. She gasped. Nestled inside were a dainty tiara and matching earrings—both with enough sparkle to light half of London. Her breath whooshed out. She could not accept these.

It didn't take a genius to piece together who had sent them.

Closing the lid with a gentle snap, she placed it beside the other boxes. She selected the next parcel, tearing away the wrapping to reveal a soft beige shoebox with gold lettering. She ran a hand across the top of the box, its sueded texture a contrast to the smooth and easily recognisable logo.

He'd sent her jewels and now Jimmy Choos?

Her heart stumbled with joy as she lifted the lid. Fine French lace in snow white covered the perfect almond-toe front. Delicate straps criss-crossed over the ankle, the buckles embedded with Swarovski crystals. They had a smooth leather heel, which looked to be a comfortable eighty-five millimetres. Which meant he'd either paid someone to put thought into this or he'd done it himself.

They were stunning—perfect wedding shoes. Just what she'd have chosen for herself.

Going through the other boxes revealed an array of perfumes, lingerie, and silk pyjamas with a matching robe. She frowned. He'd sent everything she'd need on a wedding day, except a dress.

A comment from Eva floated into her mind, about her need for a dress. Had Felix talked Eva into that? Her stomach dipped at the thought. This was ... a lot. The reality of the situation weighed on her in a way she hadn't previously acknowledged.

Lips pursed, she snapped a quick photo and messaged Felix.

'Lovely surprise to arrive home to. Why have you done all this?'

Three little dots appeared immediately.

'Just because it's going to be an intimate and secret wedding doesn't mean it's any less important. I want you to feel every bit the princess you're about to become. My princess. P.S. I need your ring size.'

Sophia's head spun and her stomach swirled like water down a drain. She sat down hard on the edge of the bed. Ring size? Seeing these items now brought home exactly what she was planning to do. Her eyes fluttered shut, fear threatening to envelope her. *No!*

She wouldn't live her life this way anymore. No second-guessing. No hiding behind a façade.

Felix had made a promise to her; she believed he meant it. She knew he'd changed. Now it was time for her to show that to him.

'I'm a size 6. And thank you. This means a lot. Xx'

Deep breaths, Sophia. She went to type more, to say something of her feelings, but held back. Dots appeared, bobbling across her screen. After a minute, they disappeared.

Trying not to ponder that, she slipped off her current heels and tried on the wedding shoes. They fit like a dream: the soft leather interior moulded to her foot. She'd easily walk in them for hours without her feet hurting. She'd need to book a mani-pedi and hair appointment. The swirling in her stomach threatened to become much more. *Deep breaths.* She might be trying to embrace this idea but perhaps baby steps would be best.

She'd go see Rachel, find out how much money she needed to come up with and how to make that work with everything that was about to go down. Her charity always gave her a pleasant feeling of calm, and right now, calm sounded really good.

13

---

*M*onday morning bloomed bright and surprisingly sunny. There was barely a cloud in the sky and for some reason that seemed a positive omen to Sophia.

Her mother was planning to spend the day at a spa—Sophia had checked her diary last night—Cynthia's first appointment was at nine. If she timed it right, she'd be able to avoid even seeing her mother today.

The day she got married.

Flicking a quick look at her watch, it was already after eight. She prayed her mum had already left.

Staying up until three going through paperwork and plans with Rachel, looking through all the legal advice they'd been given, had taken its toll on her body. At least it seemed like everything was in order. Once she secured the money from her aunt—she felt a slight pang and sent a silent message to her aunt, hoping she was okay with this—she'd give the go-ahead for work to start. She would pay the up-front payments to lock everything in for this new project.

Which meant all she had to think about today was the wedding.

Marrying Felix.

Rolling over in her bed, she buried her face against the cushioned softness of her pillow. It was her safe haven. When she'd agreed to this it had all seemed so easy. Now she worried about every little thing going wrong. What if her shoe broke? What if her mum hadn't left and wants to know what she's doing? What if someone sees them and tells Cynthia? What if she loses her voice?

What if Felix changes his mind …

Her phone rang, Eva's name flashing on the screen.

"Hello?" her voice croaked.

"Please don't tell me you're unwell?" Eva's horrified tone came through the other end.

"No, only just woke up. Sorry."

"Phew. Izzie and I are downstairs. I need you to buzz us through."

It took a moment for Eva's words to register. "Downstairs?"

"Yes. And could you hurry? This dress weighs a tonne."

The phone disconnected. Sophia's hand dropped to her side. *Dress.*

She whipped out of bed, threw on her silk dressing gown and ran to the intercom, buzzing in her friends through the intercom.

Breathing was a struggle as she waited for them to arrive at the top floor via the private lift.

The door opened to reveal Izzie and Eva holding either side of a dress rack containing one item that was hidden from view in a pristine white bag.

"What's that?"

"Good to see you too, lovely." Izzie rolled her eyes and

leaned in to kiss Sophia's cheek. "'Bout time you and Felix got your act together."

"I beg your pardon?"

Eva repeated the move, adding a small hug As she stepped back she pulled Izzie into a squeeze at her side "Izzie is a little hungover but what she means is that she's excited to welcome another fabulous woman to the family."

Sophia scrunched her eyes tight, blocking out the grinning duo before her and hoping to bring a small semblance of focus to her brain. It was spinning out at the sight of the garment bag.

A zipper being drawn had her eyes springing open, her gaze immediately locking to the noise. Each prong revealed an ounce of snow-white dress. Silk organza layers, one over the next creating an intricate V, were revealed first. A fine embroidered belt sat at the waist with delicate layers falling from it. It was simple yet elegant and Sophia couldn't wait to try the dress on. It was just perfect. She'd worn her fair share of outstanding gowns that drew gazes wherever she went. She'd worn dresses so heavy with beads she'd thought she'd topple over. She'd worn pieces that threatened to expose her figure with a wrong move.

This dress was unlike any of those.

"You said it weighed a tonne." Sophia struggled to shift her eyes from the gown before her. It was exquisite.

"I just wanted to hurry you up. Figured that might do the trick."

It had. This dress looked relaxed, almost ethereal. She reached out, stroking the fine silk as a tear slipped down her cheek. It was perfect. She'd never expected perfect.

"Tears. Not a good sign ..." Eva winced.

"No!" Sophia spun to her friend. Closing the gap with

two quick strides, she flung her arms around the shorter woman. "It's perfect. I just ... this all seems far too ... easy."

She stepped back, her arms still loosely on Eva's shoulders.

Izzie joined their huddle, throwing arms around them both. "Enough of that. I've heard marrying is the easy part. Try living with Felix—that'll be the hard bit." Izzie winked, but there was a glow in her eyes that Sophia didn't miss: happiness and satisfaction.

It was as if her heart slotted into its right place. For once everything seemed like it would be okay. She was going to get everything she needed. And as a bonus, Felix was waiting for her. She'd never wanted love, nor marriage, but for him she'd make the exception.

She might have made the offer to marry Henrik all those months ago, but it had always felt wrong. This felt right in a way she'd never thought possible.

"Marrying and living with Felix is everything I never knew I wanted. Or needed."

Speaking those words brought more tears to her eyes. She was finally free.

Felix's heart literally stopped in its chest. "Can you say that again, George?" His voice was hard. *This could not be happening.*

"There's been a hiccup with the paperwork."

"Yes, I heard that bit. It's the bit after I'm having trouble with."

"You're married, Your Highness. Already."

Felix swallowed. The saliva in his mouth had been

replaced by sawdust. This wasn't happening. This was some joke.

"How ..." His drunken week in Vegas slammed into his mind, dredged from the depths of his memory. He'd gone there after his mother's funeral. He'd gone to forget ... well, everything. "We filed the annulment papers. I signed them. They were processed."

"It would appear not. Not in America they weren't. I can get them pushed through but it will take another week, maybe two."

Felix slumped against the wall of the city registry office, his knees giving out as he slid to the ground.

He'd stuffed up. Big time.

His past was coming back to bite him on the arse. All the work he'd done on winning Sophia's trust, promising her he could solve her problems, and he was full of crap. He'd promised her he'd changed.

He couldn't marry her now. Not knowing he'd be committing a felony, dragging her along with him. It would come out. These things always did.

He'd be letting her down.

How could he not have followed that up?

Man, he was such an idiot. He couldn't even remember the other woman's name ... Amy? Or Andrea? It had been one night, one mistake. They'd both walked away without a backwards glance. And now his stupidity could cost Sophia her chance to get what she really wanted.

His actions would probably cost *him* Sophia.

Black polished shoes appeared in his periphery. "Why are you slumped on the floor like that? Oh no ... The girls, they aren't—"

"No one's been in an accident, no."

"Then, why?"

"I'm legally still married." He found the balls to look up at his brother.

Confusion mocked him in the form of Henrik.

"When did you get married?" Henrik's voice pitched. Had he ever heard his brother sound like that? The level of disbelief in his brother's tone hit him like a sledgehammer.

"Just after Mum's funeral. I was paralytically drunk; we thought it was funny. It wasn't until the next day that I found the certificate stating it was a legit ceremony. I came home and George arranged the paperwork. It was dealt with and I didn't give it another thought. At least, I thought it was."

"What will you tell Sophia?"

"The only thing I can—the truth. Can you call Eva? Have her meet us at our hotel. I don't want to do this here."

Henrik turned to his bodyguard who stood a little way behind them. "Frank, we'll need the car back please."

Felix watched the tall, lanky man speak into his phone then nod.

Henrik offered his hand, helping pull Felix to a standing position. His world tilted, like he'd been sucker punched in the face and stomach. How on earth did he go about fixing this? He'd been so cocky and sure that he could win Sophia, talk her around. He'd imagined her delight, had heard it in her voice when she'd called to thank him properly for the gifts. The engagement ring and wedding band he'd had handcrafted just for her were burning a hole in his pocket but it was all useless. His past actions had come back to kick him right where it hurt.

A hand clamped on his shoulder, giving him a little shake. "I'll take care of it. We'll make sure you and Sophia have privacy."

All Felix could do was nod.

Sophia was confused when the car drove them in the direction of The London—the hotel of choice for the Stenish royals when they stayed in town. When Felix had messaged to say he'd found a place, Sophia hadn't expected it to be the royals' private London abode. She'd assumed they'd go to a city registry office.

Upon reflection, this was a much better option. The chances of someone recognising her or Felix in a public place was high. Here they could be assured complete privacy.

Alighting from the vehicle, she received another surprise when it was Henrik who opened her car door.

"Found yourself a new job?" she asked.

"Not exactly." He grinned but Sophia noticed a fleck of ... was that worry in his eye?

"Is something wrong?"

"You should head up. Felix's waiting. We'll be there shortly."

Sophia pursed her lips. Something was off. She couldn't put her finger on it but Henrik had clammed up so her only option was to go forward.

The doorman opened the door with a bow and flourish. Sophia giggled, unable to help herself at all the pomp and ceremony. Given she'd never put much thought into how her wedding would look, this was turning out to be quite enjoyable.

She swept into the building, enjoying the light and airy feel of her dress as it floated along behind her. Her hair was pulled into intricate braids woven around each other in a loose and whimsical fashion. The tiara sat daintily on her head, the earrings occasionally clashing against her neck.

She'd never felt more beautiful and it had nothing to do with what she wore and everything to do with how alive she was inside.

When she arrived at the top floor, the door was open. A lone bodyguard stood outside, giving her a short nod but not meeting her eyes.

Okay. Odd. Not even a smile?

She'd expected to find Felix with the celebrant or whomever he'd arranged to complete the ceremony. But there was only one man.

Felix stood looking out over the city, his back to her. His shirt was strained between his shoulder blades, his hands shoved in his pockets. His broad shoulders and lean body called to her. She'd fallen asleep each night dreaming of him since their night together. His stance now left her wondering if that would be a one-time thing.

Would this be the moment that Felix turned and told her he'd made a horrible mistake? That he wasn't cut out for commitment after all? This had seemed far too easy ... Tiny prickles of fear popped along the hairs on her arms. A hair-line fracture appeared in her heart.

Was this when he reverted to his true colours?

She held her breath as his head half turned. He seemed to collect himself before he spun fully to face her. His face was a mask but his eyes drank in every inch of her.

"You look incredible, Sophia."

His words almost brought her undone. She knew in her gut something was wrong. Gone was the delight that had plagued her from the moment Eva and Izzie had walked into her home, revealing this beautiful dress. One look at Felix had doubts filling her every pore. "You're not going to marry me. Are you?" She forced the words out. Her hands fell limp to her sides. Her breathing had accelerated, waiting for a reply she didn't want, but had to hear.

"I—no. I can't."

"Can't? Or don't want to?"

He stepped towards her, holding a hand out but Sophia jolted backwards. He halted at her movement. "I need to explain."

Sophia desperately wanted to cover her ears and pretend this wasn't happening, like she used to when she was five and didn't want to do as she was told. How ludicrous was that? *You're pathetic.*

It was that thought that propelled her forward. She would hear him out; he owed her an explanation. Taking care not to touch Felix, she selected the single armchair. Gracefully lowering herself into the leather seat, she crossed her arms across her chest. She didn't say a word, waiting for Felix to explain. Waiting for him to deliver the words that would shatter her dreams into a million pieces.

"I'm already married."

It was a blow, though one she didn't let him see. She formed fists with both hands, creating physical pain with her fingernails to replace the emotional pain that was knocking at her soul. "That's certainly a vital detail to leave out." Her words were clipped and carefully chosen.

He moved towards her but she gave a small shake of her head. He sat across from her instead, leaning forward on his knees, his large hands clasped together, his eyes imploring her to hear him out. "I didn't know until this morning that it was still valid. The annulment paperwork got stuffed up. I can fix it but it's going to take at least a week."

A week she didn't have. She was out of time. In four days she turned thirty-one.

"I *can* fix this." His voice was urgent.

She swallowed, begging her body not to let the tears flow that burned behind her eyes. She was sure he *could* fix it. And she was sure he'd do everything in his power to do so quickly. But it wouldn't be enough. She didn't have time on her side.

Her body ached. Her head ached. Every part of her wished this wasn't happening.

And to top it off, her heart broke. Not because she'd lose the money. But because she'd just lost the last bit of hope she'd had left.

How could Felix possibly change? Who the hell had she been kidding? This was who he was. It was who he'd always been and Sophia needed to bring that fact back to front and centre before she got herself involved any deeper. He had married someone else and hadn't even bothered to mention the fact. He was the one who had been claiming he wanted a future, but deep down, did he really? Surely if he'd really wanted this he'd have told her everything. Who filed annulment papers and never followed up to check if they'd gone through?

How could she trust him after this?

The night they'd had together... she'd changed. She'd really placed her trust in him, but for what? Disillusion flooded her frame, hardening her heart at what was to come.

For a fleeting moment she considered begging him to marry her anyway—legal consequences be damned. She swallowed back the acid that rose in her throat. How could she possibly consider that? She was in too deep. Far too deep. Time to lock the key on her heart before any more of it escaped. "Why did you even start any of this?"

"What do you mean? You know why I've been doing this. I love you."

Her eyes fluttered shut at those three little words. Why did he have to say that to her *now*?

Don't break down. You must remain strong.

"Do you though? Or do you just think you do? You've never been able to explain why you had this sudden change in heart. Why did you want to give up your playboy ways? Why did you choose me?"

"I don't know, okay? I just know that I *love* you." He inched forward in his chair, as if he was going to take her hand. She stood, walking around the chair and over to the glass windows. If he touched her, she didn't know if she could remain immune. But she had to see this through.

The marriage didn't matter now. She wouldn't allow him to shackle himself to her on a misguided reason. In a matter of days, she turned thirty-one. It was too late for marriage and getting the paperwork sorted. She'd simply have to choose another path. One that didn't include Felix. He'd broken her trust. This news ... it just proved that she didn't deserve this type of happiness. The world was telling her that it wasn't meant to be.

Perhaps it was time she told her mother what she thought anyway and lived with the consequences. Wasn't that what this had been about all along? Her getting her freedom? It was time to grow up and break this pattern, regardless of the consequences.

She'd find another way to bring in money for the charity.

She'd find a job.

She'd find the strength to walk away from her mother and her controlling ways once and for all, and she'd do so all by herself.

Turning back from the ceiling-to-floor glass expanse, she wrapped her arms about her middle. It was time to be brutal. "I don't *want* love in my life. I don't *want* a relationship. I don't want to fall for someone. You're standing there, asking me to trust you, to believe in you, and you can't even explain your change of heart to yourself. How do you expect me to trust you won't make another sudden about-turn and go back to fooling around? What then? You say your feelings are invested now but I just don't know that I can trust they really are. I can't risk putting my heart on the line, in a position to get crushed. I have witnessed what that does to a person. I will not do it to us."

Felix's face blanched, his torso physically deflating as he sat back in his chair. He stared at her with confusion and hurt spread across that handsome face. She wanted to recall the words but wouldn't allow herself to. This was best for everyone.

Felix's voice was low and strained. "Love is about trust. You either trust my word, trust in me, or you don't. I don't have any other answers for you. I have done everything in my power these past few weeks to show you I'm serious about us. What more do you want from me?"

"I don't know." She glanced to the ground then stood up straighter. "No, that's not true. I want you to walk away. I don't need your help now."

"Are you kidding me?" His voice broke with frustration. "You refuse to see what's in front of you. You refuse to get out of your own way and admit that you already love me back. Why won't you admit that?"

His words hit home in a way she didn't want to face.

I'm scared. I'm scared of what that will do to me. Scared of the power that gives you over me.

"I'm on the brink of getting out of a lifetime of feeling powerless over my life, yet you're asking me to jump back into the deep end?"

He forged to his feet but didn't move towards her. "Love isn't meant to be about giving someone else complete power. My feelings for you aren't new, Sophia. I've had them for what feels like my entire life. All that changed is that I decided to finally do something about it. I finally feel like I'm man enough to show you I'm the real deal. If I make a promise to you, I will not break it."

"Except you already did." Her words were quiet, her voice breaking as tears started to fall like raindrops down her cheeks. They would not be contained. "Not on purpose, I know. But the marriage thing? Have you any idea how much my hopes had risen over that? Felled by the fact you *forgot* you'd already married some tart in Vegas? I mean, if we want to paint a stereotypical playboy man—let's just save us all some time and take your picture."

He stepped back like she'd slapped him.

"What will it take to prove to you I love you?" he asked. His hand lifted, clutching at thin air and then dropped back to his side.

"Nothing. It will take nothing. I do not want your love. I just want you to go."

Felix couldn't move. His body refused any command he gave it. Her last words had bruised, each taking a bite out of his heart.

"Okay. If you won't go, I will. Please do *not* follow me." The last she said over her shoulder as she started towards the door.

"Wait. Take the ring." On autopilot he walked to her, pulling the velvet box from his pocket and holding it out to her.

She paled looking at the box. "I can't accept that."

"Please. Sell it. Use the money to buy you some time. I know I've failed you, but let me think I'm doing something."

Gingerly she took the box, as though it might bite her. She caught his eye for a moment then glanced away. The hurt and desolation broke him. He'd never hated or regretted his past decisions before, but right then every single moment of those choices weighed a tonne, dragging his soul into depths of despair.

Her head bowed, she walked out of the room. He heard her quiet footsteps, the guard saying something to her, the sound of the lift opening and then doors shutting. Doors that shut as his future walked away. Without him.

He'd done this. How stupid of him to believe he could change anyone's opinion of him. Especially Sophia's, which meant so much more than anyone else's.

Would anyone ever take him seriously? He'd created this illusion of being the playboy prince, the guy who had all the fun, the man without a care in the world. And now it had stuck like glue.

He walked towards the bedroom suite he'd claimed as his own whilst staying here. He'd booked surprise flights to the Caribbean for three nights. It was all he could clear from his schedule at that moment but he'd pulled every string possible to make it work. He had wanted them to have some time together, just them, to work out how they'd play this. Felix had planned to tell her of his true feelings. He'd had vows written that he'd say to her when it was just them. He was going to pledge his heart, not just to get her the money she needed, but to show her he wanted forever. He was in this forever.

Now he'd thrown those three words at her in desperation and she'd tossed them back in his face like a dirty rag.

His black Armani overnight bag sat packed on the pristine white bedspread. It mocked him, reminding him of the dreams he'd just completely destroyed.

Screw it.

He snatched the bag off the bed and marched out the door, not giving anything a second glance.

If this is what everyone thought of him already, he may as well go with it.

14

*S*ophia stepped out of the lift and dashed straight through the front door of the exclusive private hotel. She ignored the calls of her name that sounded behind her which she assumed were from the front-desk manager. She just kept walking. It didn't matter that she was dressed in a wedding dress that was more beautiful than anything she'd ever imagined. Or that she wore shoes bought by a man she'd fallen in love with.

How the heck had she allowed that to happen?

Look at her dad—a man in love who had no idea that he was being manipulated and cheated on—on a daily basis! Love made you blind to someone else's faults. Except she wouldn't let it blind her. She was walking away, her head held high and her eyes wide open.

It was time to confront her mother and end this unhealthy control she had over her life. She'd be letting people down, but right now she needed to put herself first. Once she was free, she'd find a way to get back on her feet. She'd build up funds for the charity some other way. It wouldn't be easy, but surely there would be people out there willing to help, those outside her mother's influence.

It was time she told her father what was going on. She'd watched him moon over her mother for years—a fool in love. It broke her heart that she'd be causing him hurt, but surely it was better to know than not.

That would take away the last lie that was holding her within the supposed perfect family unit she'd been raised in.

More tears threatened, but she willed them away. She bit her lip, the sting drawing her focus. People were pointing, a few raising phones to snap pictures. She was gaining attention but with no wallet, no money, she had no choice. Hell, she didn't even have her phone. All those items were left in the limousine with Eva and Izzie.

She'd have to tell them the truth. They'd offer their help and support without a doubt, but Sophia wouldn't accept. She couldn't see Felix again anytime soon. Walking away from him had been the hardest thing she'd ever done.

Felix would realise in time he'd been making a mistake offering to marry Sophia—this way he was free to continue his life the way he really wanted. Not base his future on some spur-of-the-moment decision that he couldn't even pinpoint.

She turned a corner, hugging her torso tight to hold herself together until she was alone. Then she could break down properly in peace. The walk from the hotel to her own apartment was not far, for which she was grateful. Though the shoes really did feel amazingly comfortable—even after striding her way around the streets of London—she didn't want to be wearing this outfit anymore.

Only Felix would have thought to find her heels that looked amazing and felt beautiful.

Stop thinking about him.

Because that was so simple.

The last turn had her reaching her destination. She jogged up the steps and into the foyer. She waved a hand to the familiar security man but didn't stop to talk. She just wanted to get to her room and be alone.

The lift was blessedly empty, and she finally she could breathe without prying eyes taking in her every movement. Now was the time to map out what she'd do next. Gone were her original plans. Without the money, she couldn't maintain the charity but they had some money in their coffers. That would give her maybe a month to work out how to go forward. But first step first; it was time to tell her mother her true feelings.

After entering her pin into the keypad, she pushed in the front door.

Her brain registered the two figures standing there in the living room before her body did, stalling in the entry.

"Where have you been? And what the hell are you wearing?"

Her mother's high-pitched tone was an assault on her ears. Her father sat at the plush couch, reclined with a coffee cup held in one hand, his other arm along the top. Cynthia appeared to have been pacing in front of the lounge, her stance stiff and unyielding.

"Hi, Dad. Mother. Didn't you have a spa appointment?"

That earned her a steely eyed glare. "Where, Sophia?"

It was that command that snapped the last thread of her patience. Enough was enough.

"Nowhere that matters now. But whilst you're both here, I need to tell you I'm moving out. No longer will I be a prisoner in this family."

Lady Cynthia trilled, a laugh that grated more than nails

on a chalkboard. "Oh, don't be so dramatic. You're not a prisoner. You're clearly in a mood."

"I'm not in a mood. I'm finally coming to my senses. I turn thirty-one in four days, and no more will I live here under your roof. I appreciate everything you've given me, but now it's time for me to find some freedom in my life."

"Don't be stupid. You won't survive a minute without my money."

"That's where you're wrong. I'll be perfectly capable of living without your money. In fact, I don't want it." The moment she said the words, something clicked inside. She might have taken this life for granted, but had she ever really enjoyed it? *No.* She'd stuck around hoping that her mother would change, but she never would. "I'll be fine with friends until I can find a job."

"Ha! You have no qualifications. And I'll make sure none of your friends help you out."

"I don't have qualifications? I think setting up a successful charity and saving kids' livelihoods gives me plenty of street credit. I don't think you're really listening to me, Mother. I don't need the top job. I just want any job. Anything that will pay a minimum wage so I can start living life on my own without your interference and condescending comments over every single move I make. And I'm not talking about the friends you selected for me—I'm talking about my true friends. Those who don't care who you are."

Her mother gaped at her, disbelief shining in the ice-blue eyes that were so similar to her own. Sophia swung to her father who hadn't said a word. He took a sip from his mug.

He must have sensed it was his turn to comment. "You

don't need to be rash, sweetheart. I'm sure if you want to move we can sort something out. Can't we, Cynthia?"

"No, Gregory. We cannot work *something out*. If she's so determined to walk away then let her. She'll come crawling back."

If her mother tilted her nose any higher she'd be looking at the ceiling.

The thought gave her a modicum of amusement, which right now was a relief from the turmoil blazing inside her. Today was one for the ages as far as emotional blows went.

"I'll always be your daughter, Mum. But it's time you treated me as such, not just your toy to be played with and tossed aside when you're annoyed. I won't be crawling back. Money and status aren't crucial to me, like they are to you. I'm sorry I've never been the daughter you wanted, but I just feel there are more important things in life. That's why I started my charity, and why I've kept this up for so long but I can't anymore. I'm done." She opened her mouth to say something about her mother's affairs but then closed it. She flicked her gaze to her father, then back to her mother.

"Oh, go ahead," Cynthia snapped. "Tell him you know of my fooling around. He's known all along and doesn't bloody care."

Sophia's knees buckled. *Dad knows?* Her jaw dropped. Her limbs felt slack with disbelief. Her eyes swivelled, taking in the relaxed pose of her father which had barely shifted.

He scrunched his nose and shrugged. "One does what one does for those we love."

She closed her eyes, dipping her head. His words were another slap to the face. What the hell was wrong with him? This wasn't love! This was hideous and lying and ... *none of my business.*

What a complete mess. Yet again the ground under her feet cracked as her world changed.

"Why are you wearing a wedding dress?"

Her gaze flashed open. Her father's words brought her focus back to the pair of them. Her mother was still standing, shaking with a subtle anger that she was trying not to show. Her father drained the last of his cup before leaning forward to place it on the coffee table. Both stared at her.

"I was going to get married today." She went to add the information about how she'd found out about Agatha and the inheritance but stopped herself, offering a slight shrug instead. "I changed my mind."

"Wait! Who were you going to marry?" Her mum's face was comical—shades of beetroot came to mind—her voice shrill.

"Prince Felix of Stenaco."

Felix felt the heat of the Caribbean sun beating down on his bare chest. He'd switched his phone off. He didn't want to answer any more questions. He was the playboy prince. Known for being unreliable. He may as well make the most of that image since it seemed to be the only thing that stuck. The queasiness in his gut was probably just hunger.

He meandered along the boat ramp, catching sight of the three-hundred-foot superyacht: the ultimate luxury party set to cruise the ocean around the islands. His friend who owned it had been surprised to hear from him given they hadn't been in touch for almost a year, but it hadn't stopped him issuing Felix with an open invitation.

The yacht's sleek lines called to something in him. He could almost taste the champagne and debauchery that would be on tap once he stepped onto its smooth surface. His footsteps faltered. Even from this distance he heard the hum of a dance beat, and saw a handful of half-naked women leaning against the top railing. There was a pristine azure pool up there, offering heavenly delights and all manner of ways to put any and all thoughts out of his head.

Sophia's face swam in his mind: her shattered expression, the look of hope dying in those expressive eyes.

He couldn't take another step. His legs wouldn't budge, ignoring any command made of them.

But was this who he really wanted to be?

He slung his hands on his hips, the sun glinting off his aviators. He wasn't hungry. The queasiness had nothing to do with his food intake and everything to do with how wrong this all was. From the moment he'd boarded the plane, the first-class seat beside him glaringly bare, he'd experienced a loss inside that he'd only suffered once before in his life. This was a different type of grief to be sure, but it hurt like hell all the same.

He didn't want to be here, not like this. He'd wanted to be here with Sophia—to walk the streets, holding hands and showing the whole world that he had fallen in love with the most beautiful woman he'd ever had the pleasure of knowing—that she'd chosen him.

From the second he'd decided to come, he'd had this tightness in his chest, this feeling of ... guilt. He needed to go back to London, or wherever Sophia now was, and fight.

Why the hell did I let her walk away?

He'd so easily believed that he'd failed her, and in turn shown her that he wasn't worth trusting. All this effort and time, all his words to her that he wanted to commit and turn this into something serious—then one small hiccup led him to just give up and leave?

She'd said she didn't want his love. Well too bad. She mightn't want it. But giving up now was the wrong choice. Now was the time to prove to her the sort of man he really was, and that he wouldn't give up on her so easily.

So she had terrible views on love and marriage. He'd just need to show her that with him, it would be different. He'd spend the rest of his life proving to her that he loved her no matter what. And eventually he'd win her over.

Or wear her down.

As long as she knew that he was offering his love with no strings attached, with no pressure to be controlled by him or anyone else. She could have his love with all the freedom she wanted. She deserved to know he'd go to those lengths. He'd go to any lengths to prove he loved her. Just her.

The woman she'd always been.

Which meant right now he had to go shift mountains, and get himself legally free to marry her.

Sophia sat on her bed cradling one hand in the other within her lap. Her head was dense, like the world had been tilted sideways and she hadn't quite caught up. Her father had known about her mother?

All these years she'd shied away from real relationships, from allowing any man to get too close to her.

She'd lived her life based on what she lived at home and today it finally sunk in how far off the track she'd gone.

Her mother was controlling and cheated. Her father was in love and didn't care.

She'd always thought that her father's love for her mother had blindsided him into staying but that clearly wasn't true. What they had was what worked for them.

It would never be okay for her, but did that mean she should continue to run scared from any opportunity because she was afraid of having feelings?

Wasn't that why she'd really walked out on Felix?

She'd always equated love with being controlled but now she knew that wasn't true.

Felix had been honest with her. He hadn't tried to control her, or lie. All he'd done since the day she'd boarded the royal private jet was help her. On her terms.

He'd offered easier paths. And other than hiring a private investigator because he'd known she was running out of time, he'd only done what she'd asked.

And she'd pushed him away.

He was the one man who'd truly threatened to shake her resolve, who'd broken through and made her fall, and she'd run.

Her eyes slammed shut as she tried to keep her tears at bay. It was a useless strategy. They refused to be corralled, flowing like a silent river down her cheeks.

With no one around to watch, Sophia let herself fall apart, mourning the loss of Felix's love that she desperately wanted and had thrown away.

The following day, Sophia woke on Rachel's sofa. She had cried enough tears to fill the River Thames and could only hope that was all she had in her.

Rachel had been a godsend, insisting on Sophia staying with her the moment she'd called her friend to confess the whole mess. Her only question had been to ask why it had taken Sophia this long to walk away.

She'd told herself she'd stayed for the charity—the children—but it was more than that.

Her mother probably loved her, in her own way, but the way she'd treated Sophia was not normal. Where was the strength that Sophia had in spades for other aspects of her life? After soul-searching into the early hours of the morning, the only reasonable explanation that Sophia had come up with was her own sense of self-worth. Deep down, she'd started to believe she had to stay with her mother. She'd believed the belittling words, that she'd not survive on her own, that she needed her mother.

God. What a fool she'd been.

A knock at the door surprised her. Rachel had left for work earlier. Maybe it was a delivery though?

Standing and wrapping the cotton blanket about her shoulders for modesty, she passed across the tiny living room to the front door.

Opening it revealed not a delivery man, but Izzie. "You're a tough cookie to track down."

"Izzie!" She flung her arms around the other woman, uncaring that her blanket fell to the ground. She was standing in her skimpy pyjamas and could easily be seen from the busy street out front. "What are you doing here?"

"We figured you might need your phone and wallet?"

"No point for the phone until I can put credit on it. My mother told me she'd close my account. Given how livid she was when I walked out, I have no doubt she's gone right ahead with that threat. I appreciate you bringing them though."

"So it's true then—you're not going back?"

"Not even for all her millions. I'm done. I'm too old to play her games. It's just pathetic. I'm pathetic."

"Uh, *no*. You're not pathetic. You're caring, and lovely,

and far too nice. She's your mother, your family. It was never going to be an easy decision."

There was a haunted look in Izzie's eyes that Sophia didn't miss.

"What do you plan to do? You know you're welcome to come to Geravia and stay at the palace. It's always been like your second home."

Sophia felt the pang of those words right down to her bare feet. In the space of two days, she'd essentially lost two homes.

"I'm going to stay here with Rachel for a bit. Today's agenda includes walking the streets of London until I can talk my way into a job."

"We can find you a job in—"

Sophia shook her head, cutting off Izzie's words. "Thank you. But no. I can't see him, Izzie. Not now. I just ... can't."

Izzie did a funny shake of her head, scrunching her eyes tight for a moment. "He's not in Stenaco. No one knows where he's gone. He's pulled one of his disappearing acts."

Sophia's heart chugged to a stop. She'd done this. He'd still wanted to fight for what they had and she'd shut him down, pushed away his offer of help and love. And he'd reverted to his old ways.

Sophia didn't know what was worse—the confirmation that she'd really blown things between them, or the speed with which he'd slipped back into his old self. Maybe she had been right to question what they had? Either way, it didn't matter now.

It was time to focus on her future, and that meant finding a job.

15

Two days later, with only twenty-four hours left until Sophia's deadline, Felix walked into his father's office. George had been giving him a not-so-subtle stink-eye ever since Felix had set foot back on Stenish soil. Apparently whilst he'd cleared his schedule—what with the planned matrimony and honeymoon—when word had filtered back about the desolation of those plans, George had expected Felix to front up in Geravia to resume the cancelled royal duties.

It made Felix grin a little that George was so put out. At least some things never changed.

He'd only turned his phone off for a day, or perhaps it was two. Which wasn't even unusual for him. Previously he'd done disappearing acts that lasted a few weeks. Surely his assistant should be used to this behaviour by now.

"Felix. Nice of you to return home. I hear you'd planned to get married?" King Bastian's tone was hard to pick, but if Felix had to make a guess, he'd say it held a tinge of sarcasm.

"I had, yes. And incidentally, still do. The minor hiccup has been fixed."

He'd chartered a flight to take him directly to Vegas to have the papers signed, authorised, and filed on the spot. He'd refused to budge, calling in every diplomatic favour he had at his disposal, until he'd received word that the matter had been dealt with. He was no longer legally married—anywhere in the world—but as of tomorrow he planned to be. He'd beg. Whatever it took to prove to Sophia that he was one hundred per cent invested and in love with her—that nothing would ever change his mind on that fact. *Nothing.*

"Do I want to ask?" his father drawled with an arched brow.

"No, probably not." He slumped into the chair that sat before the king's desk. It wasn't usually the most comfortable of seating but right now, Felix's eyes drooped just from having a stationary position.

"Have you slept or even showered recently?"

Have I? He snuck a quick sniff at his shoulder and winced. "I plan to, but George was insistent that you needed to see me."

"Then I will be brief. You have been different these past few months. And I had hoped that perhaps you had turned a corner. I understand life has been hard since we lost your mother." His father swallowed and Felix's heart skipped at the broken look still lurking in his father's eyes. It didn't linger, the older man clearing his throat before continuing. "However, these past two weeks you have reverted to your old ways. Henrik covered for you the day after the wedding when you disappeared, but this has got to stop. It is time for you to grow up." His father's steel-grey eyes zeroed in on him, pinning him to the spot. No matter how old Felix was, it was a look that instilled equal parts fear and respect.

He sat up straight in his chair. "I have grown up, Father. And as such, I realise my behaviour hasn't been ideal, and hasn't done me or the family name any favours. I plan to ask Lady Sophia Huntington to marry me. If she refuses, then I'll do everything in my power to prove to her I won't stop until she knows I love her more than anything. If that means giving up royal duties then I'm afraid that is what I'll do. I guess it's only fair you know where I stand."

He'd expected an outburst. Perhaps a dressing down for being unreliable, for not putting the crown's best interests first.

What he hadn't expected was to see his father scratch his chin, and then beam like a Cheshire cat. "I told my father something very similar when I met your mother."

"I bet that didn't go down well."

"No, not particularly. But they are words I have never regretted saying. Even with your mother's illness ... and my not being able to help her ... I wouldn't choose differently. The time we had together was worth a thousand lifetimes. Finding love—true love—is like that. I can see in your eyes the same light I see in Henrik's, the same light I get in mine whenever I think of your mother. If Sophia doesn't see the truth in that look, then she is a fool. And we all know Sophia Huntington is no fool."

"Thank you." Felix rubbed at his jaw, scraping his skin like sandpaper. "You never talk about Mum."

"No. But I still think of her every day." He looked out the expanse of window that ran along the side of the room, his face unreadable and seemingly untouchable. "Enough of that. Go, find your true love. Perhaps shower first."

Felix stood, holding out a hand which his father clasped with a firm grip and a nod.

Walking out of his father's office, he was revived. Even having travelled halfway around the world, with copious hours spent sitting in waiting rooms and arguing with government officials, all on pitiful snippets of rest, he was on the right path. And no way would he be veering from that path unless Sophia chose otherwise.

Sophia's feet ached, which filled her with euphoria. She'd completed her third day of paid work in a row, and was bursting with a sense of achievement that she doubted would wear off soon. Today she'd turned thirty-one. And whilst she'd had a slight wobble this morning at that thought, she couldn't regret her actions.

She was still camping on Rachel's couch, and couldn't see herself being able to afford to leave anytime soon. She'd talked her way into a retail position at a high-end boutique. It didn't matter that the owner had possibly only hired her for who she was and the subsequent publicity—she was doing things on her own, and on her terms.

The pay, however, wasn't about to have her renting a flat in London. She'd tried to pressure Rachel into letting her pay some money for her lodgings, but her friend wasn't having a bar of it.

Which meant the money was only needed to feed and clothe herself. She'd left most of her things behind when she'd walked out, taking only the bare essentials. Felix's ring burned a hole against her breastbone, where she wore it on a fine long chain, hidden behind her clothing but close to her heart. She couldn't sell such a beautiful piece. Even if

Felix's wishes had been driven by wanting to help her, she couldn't part with it.

As threatened, her mother had put a stop to the next auction which meant the charity funding had screeched to a standstill. She hadn't worked out a solution to that problem but she would. Eventually.

Unlocking the front door of the minuscule London apartment, she was surprised by Rachel sitting on the couch. It was only mid-afternoon. "You're home early."

"I need to talk to you about something."

Sophia's heart sank a little. Had she overstayed her welcome already? "Okay. Just let me sit; my feet are killing me."

"I love that you used to be able to swan around in heels all day long, yet wearing flats in a retail position kills your feet."

Sophia shrugged, a soft smile on her face. "What did you want to talk about?"

"Two things. First, I know you said you didn't want to discuss the charity today, and didn't want to accept help ... but someone at work knows I know you, and they are a big supporter. Anyway, I won't bore you with the three degrees of separation, but she wants to help. Her dad is the head designer for Carlos Concuitto and they want to do a special line where proceeds go to Project R. He's approached me, wanting to talk directly to you."

Sophia's mouth dropped open. Carlos Concuitto were huge. They'd inserted themselves alongside cult brands such as Top Shop, Zara, and H&M—and their ethos was promoting ethical and sustainable clothing. They owned all their own factories and had some of the highest ratings for working conditions throughout their whole business.

"I don't know what to say." Was that her voice? Breathless and ... excited?

"Good. Then don't say anything because I have another thing. Your father called in to my work today. Apparently he's been trying to track you down but your phone is switched off."

Heat bloomed in her cheeks, her lips folding in on top of the other as she attempted an innocent look.

It didn't deter her friend. "Why is your phone switched off?"

"I haven't put any credit on it."

"Well, that's bull. I know for a fact you did, because I showed you how to do it."

Right, yes. She'd forgotten that small detail.

She sighed. She'd gone into a technology lockdown, deciding it would be the simplest way to ignore any of the fall out, speculation, and unwanted commentary she was sure was making the rounds. She'd seen one Instagram image of herself, striding in Eva's beautifully designed wedding dress, tears streaking down her cheeks, and she'd closed up shop on the social media front, unable to bare it. "I didn't want to take any of the calls coming through."

"Well, do me a favour and turn it back on. The lawyer in Ireland needs to talk to you."

"The lawyer? Why?"

"How should I know? He's been calling and emailing you for days but you're not answering. Perhaps you could turn your phone on and call? I left work early because I couldn't concentrate. Your dad tracked me to my work, Sophia. He said what this lawyer has to say to you is incredibly important. He also asked if you could call him when you're ready, whatever that means."

"Thank you. I appreciate you coming home early to let me know."

"Fab. Care to share that appreciation by getting your phone, stat? The suspense is killing me." Her friend grinned.

After searching her bag, she pressed the side of her phone, waiting for it to power back up.

Seeing the missed calls from Felix hit her hard but she scrolled past those to the lawyer's number and clicked the call back button. It rang a few times before it connected.

"Sophia?"

"Hi, Mr Livingston. My apologies. I've only just heard you were trying to contact me."

"Yes, my dear. I have news regarding your Aunt Agatha's will. I'm sorry I wasn't able to contact you directly after she passed—we weren't notified immediately. There's been somewhat of a kerfuffle given she didn't have any other family listed, and then contacting you was difficult. I believe you managed to track down Agatha's old address. The young lady there called to let me know you had stopped by?"

"I'm sorry I didn't tell you I'd tracked her down. As it happens, we were too late. She'd already passed away." Just saying those words brought a semblance of sadness on, not that that was hard these days.

"I'm very sorry for your loss. Would I be correct in assuming that as I haven't heard from you, your marital status hasn't changed since we last spoke?"

Sophia swallowed. "No."

"I'm very sorry to hear that. I had hoped that perhaps after your friend called the situation might have changed."

It took a moment for Sophia to register his words. "What friend?"

"The young gentleman you were with when you tracked down Agatha's old home."

Felix. Her brain felt mushy.

"Why did he call?"

"To clarify some information. Also to arrange some paperwork of your aunts that was found to be passed on to you. He'd left his details with the young lady after your visit. She contacted him and he contacted me so I could ensure they were passed into your care."

Sophia was only partially listening. What information could Felix have possibly been trying to clarify with the lawyer?

"There's a short note—"

"From Felix?"

Mr Livingston cleared his throat. "No, my dear. A short note from your Aunt Agatha. And a single photo, of her holding you as a baby, according to the back."

Oh, of course. "How wonderful, thank you. Would you mind reading me the note?"

"Certainly."

The shuffle of paper came through the phone before he cleared his throat. "Dear Sophia. Apologies, child, that we never met. Your mum was a spiteful so and so, but alas, you seemed to turn out okay from what knowledge I was able to glean about you. Take this money with only one request— use it for good. Don't just hand it over to your mum. Love, Agatha. It's dated from about a year ago."

It would seem her Aunt had just assumed she'd be married and that there was no question in her Aunt's mind of her not inheriting the money. Her desire to keep the money from Cynthia's clutches most likely explained the marriage stipulation. Money really did do crazy things to the women in her family. Perhaps it was for the best that she wouldn't inherit it. A single tear slid down her cheek.

Gosh, she cried easily these days. It was like years of pent-up frustration, anger, and keeping everything in check were now taking their toll, bursting forth with ease.

"Thank you," she whispered. A tissue appeared before her which she gladly accepted, dabbing at the tears.

"I'm afraid that's actually not all that was found. As it was a deceased account, I double-checked the papers just in case, and well, it would seem your aunt made another will about a month before she died. It hadn't been handed over to us to update her one on file but it is a legitimate will."

"Another will?" She didn't mean to repeat his words but she was struggling to follow.

"Yes. Another *different* will."

"Different how?"

"Unfortunately nothing to do with the marriage clause, but instead of the money being giving in its entirety to the state, half will be donated to charities around the world. She's listed them. I am sorry this wasn't better news for you."

Sophia slumped back in the armchair, blinking more than was normal at this news before a smile of pure elation spread across her face. "No. Don't be sorry. This is actually wonderful news. I never wanted the money for me. Are you able to please forward me a copy of the charity list along with the other items? I'd love to know who she's chosen to help."

"Of course, my dear."

Sophia rattled off the address of her friend and then rang off. She sat in surprised yet happy shock for a while before Rachel started waving a hand to and fro in front on her face. "Earth to Soph?"

"The money's not completely lost. And with your news from today, nor is Project R. And I have a job. I'm free!"

"Ooookay. All I heard was different will. Did you get the money after all?"

"No. But part of it will now go to charities around the world, it will make a difference in a good way. In a way that matters to people who need it most. This is what my aunt would have wanted—I'm sure of it."

"I'm still not sure I understand why she wanted you to have to marry to get it in the first place."

"My guess is that it would add another name as a claimant of the money—stop my mother getting her hands on it. I don't know. Unfortunately, I'll never be able to ask my aunt and I certainly don't plan on asking my mother."

Rachel engulfed her in a hug. It was lovely but it also shot a pang straight to her heart. She wanted those arms to be Felix's. She ached to ring him and tell him that it didn't matter, there was no silly timeframe now and it had all worked out for the best. She'd been a fool to push him away. If only she'd received this information earlier ... Without the pressure of marriage and everything that entailed, they could have just dated.

She could have given him time to follow through on his word.

Except would that still have led to heartbreak on her end?

Her heart screamed no. But her head said maybe.

He'd upped and run the minute she'd walked out.

Either way, it didn't matter as now she'd never know. She doubted she'd be seeing Felix again any time soon.

"Actually, there was one more thing. Birthday drinks. Tonight."

"I'm not really in the mood to celebrate turning another year older."

"Then we'll celebrate your emancipation from your mother's controlling ways. The amazing offer from Carlos Concuitto that saves Project R. Part of your Aunt's money going to help those in need. Take your pick, lady, but we are *going* to celebrate."

16

$\mathcal{F}$elix straightened the bow tie at his neck, feeling a little light-headed. He'd put everything on the line. Literally. He'd told his father he'd walk away from the crown if it meant a choice between Sophia and Stenaco. Hell, he'd attempt to fly to the moon if it proved to her he was a changed man.

He glanced around at the spacious yet practically bare apartment. He hadn't wanted to fill it with furniture, as he figured that might be something Sophia would want to do.

Please let her want this.

Izzie had texted, saying Sophia and her room-mate were coming up in the lift now on the pretence of birthday drinks. He flicked his wrist, taking in the time. He had exactly five hours to convince Sophia to marry him. If not for love—even though he planned to reinforce his own love for her—but to secure her future happiness.

When he'd contacted the lawyer to forward the paper-work that had been found, he'd checked the terms of the bequest. Sophia only had to show the signed marriage certificate with any date before or *on* the day of her turning thirty-one. Which meant if she signed tonight, and married him, then she could get her money still. He'd stick by her for as long as she'd allow and he'd show her he was the real deal. She would have to be the one to walk away from him. Deep in his gut he knew she wanted this—that she also loved him. She was just scared.

He understood that. But time would prove him right, and if they had to remain married for five years, well, that sure gave him time.

The door handle jiggled, and Felix tensed. Her laugh reached him before he saw her. The combination relaxed every bone in his body, like the feeling he got when he listened to the opening bars of his favourite song and was transported to another world.

Showtime.

He knew the exact moment she saw him. Her body stilled, and he heard her quick intake of breath.

"Sophia."

Her name felt right coming from his lips. Looking at her, everything fell into place. Sleepless days of travel and fighting and pleading with American government officials were nothing if it meant he got this right.

Her eyes darted to her friend, brows narrowing. Unspoken words passed between the two and Felix could only wait, hoping against hope that she wouldn't just turn around and storm out.

Her shoulder twitched and she made a minuscule shift back towards the door.

"Please." He held up a hand, not daring to move closer. "Hear me out."

Her friend clasped a hand to Sophia's arm, giving it a gentle squeeze, and then spun her towards Felix and pushed her forward. She then walked right back out the door she'd just come through, leaving Sophia and Felix alone.

"Did you orchestrate this?"

"Yes."

"Why, Felix? I'm pretty sure we've said all there is to say. Shouldn't you be off in the Bahamas or Bora Bora?"

"Caribbean, actually. Izzie said she'd told you I'd left. And what she said was partly true. When you walked out, I didn't know what to do. So I took my bag and I boarded the flights I'd booked for our honeymoon. I called up an old friend who's always up for a party. As I walked towards his yacht, everything just felt ... wrong. There was something missing. You."

"Felix, we've been through this. I'm not interested—"

"Stop. I'm not married anymore. I flew to America, into Vegas, and I stayed there, pulling every diplomatic string I had at my disposal and I forced the divorce to go through. I can legally marry you. All you have to do is say yes. Izzie is waiting downstairs with her celebrant licence. I checked the fine print with your lawyer in Ireland. So long as our marriage certificate is dated today, the will terms stand. We can still get you the money. I own this apartment, and the floor below. When we marry, they'll become yours. We can live here. You can expand your charity work and do all of those things you told me about in Ireland. I've told my father that if proving to you that I am serious about us and marriage means giving up my title, then so be it. He understands. He knows what lengths we need to go to for those we love."

He sucked in air, unsure if he'd taken a breath the whole time he'd spoken.

He'd expected something. A reaction of some kind, but Sophia just stared at him, her face blank, her lips slightly parted. The silence ate at him but he didn't dare break it. Her eyes seemed glazed, floating about like wispy clouds, then she blinked multiple times and they latched onto him.

She walked over until she stood right before him. "You did all of that for me?"

"I'll do more, if that's what it takes."

Never in her wildest imagination could Sophia have thought up something like this. The lengths he'd gone to, to ensure he could keep his promise to her ...

Felix stood before her and had all but bled his blue blood from his veins, promising to do what it took to prove his love for her.

"I don't need the money." The words slipped out.

His brows scrunched in such a confused fashion, she itched to stamp her thumb to the skin and smooth it out. "But your charity ... Izzie said your mum had cut off the funding."

"She has."

"Then—"

Sophia pressed a finger to Felix's lips. "We've found another source of funding for Project R. Carlos Concuitto is going to design a line where proceeds will go to the charity. I walked away from Cynthia. Her cutting off the funding hurts a little in the short term but I'm finally free of her."

"You don't want to get married? To secure the money still?"

"The lawyer called me this afternoon. The papers you had delivered to him from the woman who bought my aunt's house contained another will. Half the estate is being donated to other deserving charities around the world. I only ever wanted the money because I thought I needed it to be able to leave Cynthia's controlling ways. But that wasn't true. I walked away knowing I'd have nothing, and it's all worked out okay."

His eyes slid from hers, focusing over her shoulder. "Oh."

Disappointment was not the reaction she had expected. "I'm sorry. I know you've gone to a lot of trouble. All that travel and lost time ..." She was babbling. Why was she babbling? "You're disappointed."

"Yes and no. I'm really happy for you that things have worked out how you wanted them to from the start. You were straight with me—clear that all you wanted was the money—not the marriage. But I guess I'd hoped that the marriage clause would allow me to prove my commitment to you, my love that I still feel for you, during that time."

Sophia's heart jolted at the *L* word.

Felix hadn't upped and reverted to his old ways. At least, he'd considered it for a millisecond and then he'd gone and found a solution for her. Just like he'd promised. If that didn't show her his unwavering devotion and commitment then what did? She didn't need a five-year marriage to prove that. She didn't need any marriage at all. All she needed was him.

What barriers were left between them other than her saying those words that she'd always wanted to say but had been too scared to put out there?

He reached out and took her hand, his eyes wandering about but still not meeting hers. "It was worth it. Even if you don't need me now, it wasn't a waste. Spending time with you showed me that I had been reckless in the past, and careless with my time. I should be putting it to better use."

"I do," she whispered.

That got his attention, his focus darting straight to her. His shoulders visibly tensed and his grip on her hand tightened. "Say that again?"

"I do ... need you, I mean."

He slumped a little, but Sophia couldn't hold back anymore. She'd left him teetering long enough. Using her other hand, she fished out the ring that lay hidden down the front of her dress and pulled it over her head. Kneeling to the ground, she held it to him. "I'm not going to ask you to marry me. But I am going to ask you to take this ring back and keep it in a safe place for when we reach that stage."

"We?"

"Yes. We. You and me. I sort of thought it might be nice to just try good old-fashioned dating first."

The corners of his mouth twitched, slowly meandering into a full cocky grin. His slate-blue eyes twinkled with mischief. The Felix she'd fallen in love with was back and they were finally on the same page.

"Are you sure? Because I could totally just marry you right now. All you have to say is yes."

"You just won't give up will you?"

He pulled her from her position, into his arms. The moment she was locked against his chest, she was flooded with the true sense of happiness she'd been waiting for from the moment she'd walked out her parents' door.

"I will never give up, Sophia. I told you I'd changed, and I'm now a man of my word."

"I believe you. You are different. I think maybe I've sensed that for a while, even before we went to Ireland. I'm not sure I ever thanked you properly for all you've done."

"Well ... you know how I like to call in my debts—"

Before he could say anything else, Sophia pressed her

lips against his, delighting in their delicious warmth, feeling like she'd come home.

She lifted her lips away a millimetre, her eyes locking with his. "I love you. I'm sorry I didn't trust you the way I should have. I was wrong to use your past against you. I was scared of allowing you in, but I know now there's nothing to be scared of. Loving you doesn't mean I lose who I am. It makes me a better person."

"Not sure I can top that, so I'm just going to say, I love you too, and show off with my superior kissing skills."

He certainly had a knack for it.

Wherever the world would take them, so long as Felix was with her, she'd be strong enough to handle anything.

THE END

ABOUT THE AUTHOR

Jayne Kingsley writes contemporary romance filled with fashionable and fun heroines and the hunky heroes that capture their hearts. She currently resides on the picturesque south coast of NSW with her two young daughters and her own real-life gorgeous hero.

www.jaynekingsley.com

facebook.com/jaynekingsleyauthor

instagram.com/jaynekingsleyauthor

bookbub.com/authors/jaynekingsleyauthor

PREVIEW OF BOOK 3 GUARDING HIS RUNAWAY PRINCESS

Read on for a sneak peek of *'Guarding His Runaway Princess: The Stenish Royals Book 3'*

CHAPTER 1

*P*rincess Isabella wiped the trickle of sweat from her brow. It wasn't that hot out, but her body was slowly heating from the inside, a tell-tale sign she was about to be forced to do something she didn't want to do. But she would do it. For her father, she would do this.

Taking the last step, she entered through the side door and halted. Across the stage she could see the man in question, King Bastian, conversing with both her brothers, Henrik & Felix and their significant others, Eva and Sophia.

It was like a scene from a Hallmark movie. Happy couples holding hands whilst they laughed with the man of the hour. Her father who had no trouble giving each person who spoke his full attention—he looked each of them in the eye as he listened and answered—not an ounce of uncertainty or blame to be scene.

Something within her rolled over, another wave of heat danced down her spine. Her father never looked at her like that. He never spoke directly to her.

Had they even realised she wasn't there yet?

It was like her brain took a snapshot of the happy scene

before her, and played out the movie of what would happen if she walked forward and joined them. How her presence seemed to suck the air from the room when she and her father were both there. How, no matter what she did, he still couldn't bear to even look her way.

Today's event wasn't unusual, but having the whole Royal family in attendance was. Izzie tried to take that step, to propel her body forward towards the gathering. Her legs were lead. The heat that had been threatening drew closer, and she knew she was in trouble.

She stumbled back, Ian placing a steadying hand at her shoulder.

"Princess? Is everything all right?"

His words were comforting, but his presence wasn't. Ian had been her bodyguard since she was in nappies, and had looked after her Mother. At least he had before she'd taken her life. They'd lived through that ordeal together and she knew no matter what he'd always be there for her. Her silent father figure who comforted more than her actual father.

But not even he knew of her little problem. A little problem that was starting to become far more frequent and far more pressing.

"I have to go." Her words were breathless, air refusing to be dragged into her lungs that burned for that sweet freshness. The command to her limbs hit it's mark, finally allowing her to brush past the older yet solid form behind her, back through the door and out the back of the stage. More bodyguards stood at the entrance, giving her a short nod but not questioning her frazzled and almost drunken movements. Why couldn't she move anything properly?

It had been months since this last happened. Why now? Why today?

Her thoughts scattered as desperation to be alone taking over all else.

"Princess Isabella? Are you ill?"

Ian's voice again. His hand cradled her elbow to guide her away from the side entrance. She could hear voices calling, laughing, could smell the festive food in the air. All normal things. Maybe if she could focus on just one normal thing she could hold this at bay.

The eerie noise beckoned, her head collapsing into one giant ache. She scrunched her eyes tight, trying to block the noise with her hands over her ears like she'd done when she was four and hadn't wanted to listen to a berating.

Then her world went black.

***

She came too, her eyes taking in the pale beige carpet above her. Why was there carpet above her? *You're in a car, stupid.* The motion and whizzing sounds were unmistakable. Sitting up, she held her head. "Ouch."

The car slowed a modicum.

"Princess Isabella, you should lay back down. You blacked out, I'm taking you to the hospital."

"No! Just take me home." Silence met her request. "I mean it, Ian. Take me back to the palace. That's not a request, it's an order."

Their eyes met in the rearview mirror, his edged with crinkles of concern. She thought she caught the start of an eye roll but he glanced away.

He didn't answer, but inclined his head, indicating to turn the car around and head towards the palace. Not answering wasn't good - that meant he was angry with her.

And if he was angry with her, she could only imagine what her father would be.

But right now she didn't care. She forced herself not to. Instead she took Ian's advice and laid back down, perhaps that would help flatten his feathers a little.

That one scene back at the festival had broken her. How did seeing her family all so happy—without her—cause such a reaction. Was that even normal?

No. Of course it's not normal. That's not what brought on your anxiety attack though, is it?

She really hated her internal voice sometimes. Particularly when it was correct.

The black sedan slowed. She could hear the slight scrape and whir of the electronic gates telling her they were close to home. The car accelerated up the long driveway, the occasional blip of branches breaking her view of the pristine blue skies. She sucked in air, pleased when it didn't catch in her throat. Her lungs and throat ached from the deprivation from earlier. Her mouth felt funny, probably form the excessive short puffs she'd been doing.

Maybe Ian was correct, and she needed to go to hospital, but she couldn't. Something told her this wasn't a medical issue so much as a mental issue.

Her brain was broken.

Her emotions were screwed.

I'm a walking liability to the family.

***

Ethan Raine glared at his commanding office. Gardening leave? What the hell was this! He didn't work in some God damn office.

"Could you repeat that, Sir?"

"You're relieved of duty. Not forever, but right now you're a liability. You won't take the hints we've given you, so it's time we took action to the next level."

Ethan ground his teeth in a way that had him mentally apologising to his dentist. Instead of answering, he gave a short nod. "Understood, Sir." He stood and walked out of the room.

He congratulated himself on not smashing his fist into the wall on his way out.

Years of work brought undone by a situation out of his control.

With one more deep breath he pushed the anger aside. It would do him no good. He'd learnt that the hard way. But unlike most he never repeated a mistake twice.

He was a trained soldier, and as such, he'd do as he was trained.

Perhaps it was time to take that holiday he'd always dreamed of. Sydney in Winter was okay, but nothing to write home about. New Zealand beckoned, the idea of pristine fluffy snow and ice cold beer enough to seal the deal. If he couldn't work here then he'd darn well go elsewhere to work off his energy in another way. Queenstown was only a short flight. *Screw it.* He'd go home, book the next flight, pack a bag and his skis. This time tomorrow, with any luck, he'd be carving up some of that powder the Kiwis were bragging about right now.

***

Izzie stormed into her father's office. There he sat. The King of Stenaco.

"Not now, Isabella. I need to go over this speech for tomorrow evening."

Her father didn't so much as glance her way. *Not anything out of the ordinary there*. Well not this time, this time she'd make him hear her out.

"Yes, now, Father. When am I going to get an answer from you?"

He placed his pen back against the desk, with a subtle thud. She heard his breath exhale, as if he shouldered the weight of the world, not a simple question regarding Izzie's future.

"When I believe you're taking the situation seriously." He held up a copy of yesterday's papers, a tabloid that had a tendency to print trash, one that regrettably featured her own delirious face on the front cover. Her dress was hitched to the side showcasing her underwear and her mascara had smudged in a way that was less smoky siren and more drunk panda.

"That was taken weeks ago."

"When you were in Greece, having skipped out on tasks that were delegated to you, right after your brother's wedding. You want to be taken seriously yet you pull stunts like this?" he stabbed a finger right on the image of her face, his eyes finally looking up from his desk. Tired blue irises bore into hers, laden with sadness. He physically flinched, flicking his gaze back to the paper.

That one movement hurt worse than a bullet. Worse than the words he'd just thrown at her. It was an emotional punch she hadn't been ready for. How often had her father really looked upon her for more than a moment since her mother passed?

Her brain refused to correlate that information.

She took a seat in the chair that faced his desk.

"I know my behaviour has been bad, but I want that to change. I'm ready to get back on track. You've let enough stuff slide with Felix and at times Henrik. Why are you always so much harder on me?"

He didn't answer. The injustice was like acid on her tongue. As usual his treatment of her stood out as another dismissal of her place in his life.

After what seemed an age he sat back a little in his leather chair. "And today? Was that your idea of being ready to get back on track? Ian told me you fainted. Refused to go to the hospital. What was it this time, Isabella? Too hungover? Drugs? Drunk at eleven am when the rest of your family turned up to officially open the Summer Festival? You say you want to change but I don't believe you."

Izzie couldn't look at his face anymore. Even without eye contact, his disapproval radiated towards her. Condemning her without a chance of rebuttal. Her eyes fell to the pen that sat on top of this hand written speech. He picked it up, twisting it around before dropping it back to the table. It was practically identical to those that Henrik and Felix both had. Heavy gold with their names inscribed in flowing script along the body. Gifts from their mother only months before she ended her life.

Izzie hadn't received one.

She'd swallowed back that pain and had thanked her mother for her own gift, which had seemed to signify that even her mother didn't see her as having a serious path as part of the crown. She'd been given a makeup mirror. Gold like theirs. Her name inscribed like theirs. But the meaning clear.

She wouldn't need to be signing documents. She'd just be checking her makeup.

Fed up with waiting she pushed the chair out, the loud screech somehow pleasant compared to the loaded silence.

Marching out of the room she pulled the door shut behind her. The wood went *thunk*, creating a slight echo through the corridor.

Well booey to him.

Yes she'd acted like an immature idiot since her mother passed. She wasn't the only one! What twenty-three-year-old princess would cope okay after her mother decided to swallow a whole bottle of sleeping tablets and lay within the depths of her own especially designed rose maze, waiting to be discovered? It was like the stuff of fables.

Izzie would never recover from that sight. Finding her mother, her skin almost translucent, her body colder than ice. One touch to her hand had sent Izzie into a world of denial and pain.

Without warning her knees gave out, and she fell in a crouch, her eyes slamming shut. Her body actively repelled the memories that would appear out of nowhere, assaulting her with what would never be.

Was it any wonder she'd spent the past five years running from anything and everything?

Just like this morning, the panic mounted. Her breathing was shallow but no matter what she did she couldn't suck down deeper breaths. Her eyes blinked open, but her vision blurred, nothing making sense except an urge to flee.

What did they say about trauma victims? Fight or flight?

It didn't take a genius to work out her preference. And it didn't seem worth fighting it anymore. It was time to go away.

For good this time.

***

The plane taxied along the runway, the flight having been short and smooth. Just as Ethan liked. Flying wasn't his favourite thing. Somehow every time he stepped foot on a plane he felt helpless. No gun or bodyguard skills would help him if the plane just fell out of the sky. A ridiculous concept perhaps, but one he couldn't shake.

A dainty foot in heels, tapping to an unknown beat, caught his eye. It wasn't the first time he'd noticed her, and anticipation was coiling in his gut at the prospect of seeing what the rest of that foot led to. A flash of blonde ponytail had occasionally peeked out the side of the seat that was three rows ahead of his. The diagonal view hadn't given much away but it had entertained him for the past thirty minutes since his movie had ended. Not that Uma Thurman wasn't captivating, but something about the woman ahead intrigued him more.

For one thing, who wore three inch stiletto heels into Queenstown? It was ski season and they'd be landing late evening which meant temperatures in the negative. She appeared to be wearing skintight jeans and some sort of loopy jumper but nothing that spoke of sub-zero wear.

The plane jolted to a stop. Passengers jumped to stand even though the seatbelt signs glared their backlit message to remain seated. He mentally shrugged, in no hurry to follow the crowd. He noted Miss Stiletto hadn't stood either.

The man beside him shifted closer, and Ethan felt expelled breath against his face. Without moving, his eyes tracked to the inconsiderate idiot beside him. It did the trick, the poor dude's face paled a shade or two and he shifted back into his own personal space.

Giving it another few minutes, allowing the young

harassed mother with two whining children to stand and move off, he followed suit.

Damn. His interaction with close breath man meant he'd missed his opportunity to see Miss Stiletto stand. Never mind. He'd catch up with her at baggage claim. Or if she was already gone then it didn't matter. He was here on holidays, for once he had no one to protect, no one to investigate. Nothing but a few weeks of solid relaxation before him.

At least that's what he kept telling himself, ignoring the niggling in his gut that said otherwise.

Order your copy here!

FREE ROMANTIC SHORT STORY

Sign up to Jayne Kingsley's newsletter to stay up to date with all her latest news and special exclusive offers. She's pretty haphazard, so don't fear, you won't be inundated with emails. Signing up will get you this fun and flirty FREE romantic short story.

Newsletter sign up: https://jaynekingsley.com/sign-up/

www.ingramcontent.com/pod-product-compliance
Lightning Source LLC
Chambersburg PA
CBHW020144120726
47903CB00007B/2409